W9-BNN-368

Abe Gilman's Ending

Aunt Susie

Enjoy

Abe Gilman's Ending

A NOVEL

GLENN FRANK

BEAUFORT BOOKS · NEW YORK

FIRST EDITION

This is a work of fiction. Names, places, characters, and incidents are either the products of the author's imagination or are used fictitiously.

Library of Congress Cataloguing-in-Publication Data

Frank, Glenn, 1957–
Abe Gilman's ending : a novel / by Glenn Frank.
p. cm.
ISBN-13: 978-0-8253-0511-5 (alk. paper)
ISBN-10: 0-8253-0511-X (alk. paper)
1. Widowers—Fiction. 2. Jewish men—Fiction. 3. Long-term care facilities—Fiction. I. Title.

PS3606.R73A63 2006
813'.6—dc22

2006014418

Published in the United States by Beaufort Books, New York
Distributed by Midpoint Trade Books
www.midpointtrade.com

10 9 8 7 6 5 4 3 2 1

PRINTED IN THE UNITED STATES OF AMERICA

For Cathy, Jamie, and Mark
OWDS

GLOSSARY

Adas Yeraim: Hassidic Jewish synagogue

alte cocker: Literally, an old shit, or as we say in English, an old fart

Baruch ata adonois, elohanuh melech ha-o-lum: The first words of the main prayer said on the Jewish Sabbath meaning "Praised be Thou, O Lord, our God"

bima: The dais from where the rabbi preaches

B'nai Zion: Jewish synagogue (not quite as conservative as the Khal Anshei Chessed or Adas Yeraim)

chazzer: A pig or anyone who acts like one

chazzeri: Literally, pig slop, rotten, junk

Congregation Sfath Emes: Orthodox Jewish synagogue

golems: Monster

gonif: Thief

goyim: Non-Jews

Hadashim: Old Jewish text

Haftorah: Text selected from the Book of Nevi'im ("The Prophets") that is read publicly in the synagogue after the reading of the Torah on each Sabbath

halavai: "that's wonderful" (sarcasm intended)

Hassidic: Literally, piousness. A Jewish movement originated in the eighteenth century (very devoutly adherent to tradition)

Kaddish: Prayer for the dead

kena hora: Literally, the evil eye, said in order to ward off evil

keppele: A head

Khal Anshei Chessed: Hassidic synagogue

kugel: Noodle pudding

kvetcher: One who complains

Mazel Tov: Congratulations

mezuzah: A scroll inscribed on one side with Biblical passages and inserted into a small case that is attached to the doorpost of a home, or worn around the neck

minyan: A quorum of ten or more adult male Jews necessary for the purpose of communal prayer

mishigas: Craziness

Mishnah: The first recording of the oral law of the Jewish people (the first work of Rabbinic Judaism)

motza: Unleavened bread eaten at Passover

mumzer: A bastard

oye: Oh no

oye gutenue: Oh no, oh no

pintel: A little penis

punum: Face

rebbe: Rabbi

Rosh Hashanah: The Jewish New Year

shayna punum: Pretty face

shiksa: A non-Jewish girl

shpilkies: Literally, pins. Ants in the pants, impatience

shtetel: Village

shmata: Rags

shmuck: Literally, penis, but often used to refer to someone who's intentionally nasty

shtreimel: A fur hat worn by orthodox Jewish men

shul: Synagogue

sockeldodger: A big penis

tallis: Prayer shawl

Talmud: A record of rabbinic discussions of Jewish laws, ethics, customs, legends, and stories

tefilin: Leather cubes containing scriptural texts on parchment worn on the head and arms during morning prayers by males

Teshuvah: The forty days preceding Yom Kippur (a period designed for fixing mistakes so they will not be repeated)

tsourus: Agitation

tukhis: Rear end

tzitzit: Fringes on a garment worn during prayers

utermensch: monster (German)

Ohab Zedek: Jewish synagogue (not quite as conservative as the Khal Anshei Chessed or Adas Yevaim)

yenta: Busybody, gossiper

Yiddisha kopf: Jewish smarts

Yom Kippur: Day of Atonement

Zionist: Someone who supports the State of Israel

Abe Gilman's Ending

Nearly a year had gone by, but my room at Emunah remained as bleak and barren as the day I'd arrived. I had, at one time, thought about hanging a picture of Sarah or painting over the bleached-out square on the wall outlining where my predecessor had hung his own family portrait before he conveniently died. I never did, however. I had neither the energy nor the urgency, and since Sarah was gone, nothing seemed to matter.

My name is Abe Gilman, and when I came to Emunah I was seventy-seven years old, certain I was already dead.

Sarah wrote me a note the morning she died. *Called back* was all it said.

"Those two words held much of Sarah's spirit," the Rabbi told me at her Shiva. "There were, to her, neither challenges too great to overcome nor insurmountable odds."

We had met on a train more than fifty years earlier. I was traveling back to my boyhood home near Boston after an interview for a teaching position at Brooklyn's Fort Hamilton High School. Sarah was returning from a visit to a friend. The train, the Northeast Passenger Atlantic, was crowded.

"Would you mind sharing your table?" the dining car maître'd asked. "This young lady is looking for a seat."

She had green eyes, olive skin, and chestnut hair falling lightly across her shoulders. I also remember the freckles cascading across her nose and fading into her cheeks and the way the delicate gray dress hung loosely from her frame. She was breathtaking.

She smiled politely at me, and I stared at her neck, which to me, seemed at once sultry and graceful.

"Is it all right if I read over dinner?" I asked as she sat.

"Do you mind if I read over your shoulder? This is so dull." She lifted her own book.

I smiled as if to say I understood, but we rode on in silence — I was too shy, and smitten, to say more — and we may never have spoken again had the busboy not provided a plate of rolls that he hurriedly dropped between us.

I held the bread in the air. "Excuse me sir, do you have any motza today?"

"We ain't servin' any cheese today, fella." He turned to Sarah. "Can you read 'em the menu, honey." Then he was gone.

Sarah shook her head at my naïveté.

"It's Pesach . . . Passover," I said awkwardly. "I'm Jewish."

"I figured that out." She lifted her book so I could see the title: *Jewish Women Through the Ages* by Trude Weiss Rosmarin.

"I didn't get to the book. I couldn't take my eyes off your neck."

She looked puzzled.

"You've got a really nice neck," I stammered, revealing my ogling. "Obviously a very smart neck," I added acknowledging the tome in her lap. "But it's very nice."

With my dignity already sullied and in no further need of being guarded, our conversation flowed with increasing ease. We discussed everything imaginable into the night, and in truth, I do not recall whether we were ever served anything to eat, or even whether the train made its scheduled stops. Mayor Mansfield and the Boston Braves were mentioned, I do remember that, and, inevitably, the terrible events unfolding in Europe and Palestine, as well as our shared enthusiasm for Upton Sinclair, Jack Benny, and Duke Ellington. I believe we also considered our prospects for the future. I declared my intent to be a teacher and a writer, while Sarah expressed a desire to have children — many children — and to raise a family. Her sparkle, through the train's smoky cigarette fog, is still clear in my mind, as is how tempting it was to reach across the table and hold her hand in mine.

We were married ten months later.

A few weeks after Sarah's death, I fell and shattered my right hip.

"Abraham, you have suffered a serious fall," Dr. Glick said. "We did everything feasible, but walking again — I'm afraid there are no guarantees. In fact I think it may be unlikely. The pain will diminish, but the severe nerve damage may cause permanent numbness from your thigh to your ankle —"

"I went through a whole war and not a scratch, now I fall down a few little stairs and this?" I tried to move but a staccato burst of throbbing pierced my thigh, and I could only wince.

Mention of the war forced a memory to the surface.

> *"If you get killed over there I will kick your ass," Sarah had said to me with a tremble as I waited to board the train to boot camp. "Even your mother thought I could take you in a fair fight."*

"Well, I'll miss you too."

She laid her head against my chest. "Two children," she said. "A boy and a girl. As soon as you get back. I promise. A philosopher king and a precocious tomboy; just like we talked about."

"Good. Don't start working on it without me."

"And you, you leave the French women alone when you're over there. You'll embarrass yourself."

The train whistle sounded and we watched the other couples separate slowly.

"Tell the Rabbi to say a prayer for me," I said.

"What a world," she whispered.

Without Sarah to help me through, I was lost and helpless.

Doctor Glick was right; I couldn't walk, and I was humiliated. I couldn't do anything for myself, and my grief over losing Sarah was unbearable.

"Anyone you want me to call?" The nurse asked.

"We wanted so badly to have children," I murmured in a painkiller fog. "But she'd had scarlet fever as a child. She couldn't have children."

"That's too bad."

"She was sad for a month when we found out, but I let it go."

"That was nice of you, to be that understanding. That must have been difficult."

"She became a teacher. Like me. She just decided one day and that was it."

Her first day as a teacher filtered back to me. She was nervous and jittery.

"I don't know anything about kids," she said when I dropped her off. "They'll laugh at me."

"They're eight-years-old," I scoffed. "They don't even know how to laugh yet."

When she returned home, she was all stories and excitement.

"The boys were playing rough in the playground, so I asked them what they were doing," she said. "This one kid says: 'We're playing cops and robbers and I just robbed the Last National Bank.*' " She paused. "Of course, I'm the teacher, so I say instructively and with all my authority: 'you mean the* First National Bank.*' 'No, he says, the* Last National Bank. *I robbed all the others already.' "*

After a month, my misery alchemized into despair.

"Meet Mr. Maxwell Brody and Jennifer Kent," Dr. Glick said arriving with a group of strangers.

"I'm tired. I want to rest."

"May I call you Abraham?" It was Maxwell Brody, red-faced and egregiously overweight.

"Yes."

My mind drifted. *Sarah's Uncle Gerry was built just like Maxwell Brody — round and protruding — and once he'd arrived at our house to proudly announce he had shed five pounds.*

"That's like losing a deck chair off the Queen Mary,*" I whispered to Sarah in the kitchen.*

She choked with laughter. "That's terrible. Don't say things like that." I loved to make her laugh.

"I'm an attorney. My name is Jennifer Kent. I'm with Legal Services for the Elderly. It is our job —"

"I don't need a lawyer." I was genuinely surprised, not only because I had no idea why she was here, but also because she was so young.

"Dr. Glick doesn't feel you'll be able to meet your needs at home. We've all reviewed your status. You have no one to help you. Your home has no wheelchair access. You have only your teachers' pension to live on, and your only asset is the house. You can't afford around-the-clock nursing care."

"We're very sorry for your loss, Mr. Gilman," Brody interrupted, "I understand your wife was lovely."

"It's my job as attorney to act in the best interests of the patient," Jennifer Kent interrupted as though he hadn't spoken. "When I believe it's in the patient's best interest to receive the full health-care benefits that can be provided outside the home, even if the patient objects, I'm free to take action necessary to implement the recommendation."

I was stunned. Dr. Glick was studying charts on his clipboard and did not seem to be listening.

"What does that mean?"

"You'll have your own room," Brody broke in. "Your own space; you'll be free to come and go as you please. You'll get good meals, and above all, people will be around to help you when you need it. We help you move. We get you acclimated. This is a very positive thing. Honestly, we only want what's best."

He reached down and picked up his briefcase. "I'm from the Emunah Retirement Center and Convalescent Facility." And with that, he presented me with a brochure.

During my first weeks at Emunah, I found that, in the afternoons, with the blinds shut and the curtains drawn, I could occasionally doze off, and in that state souvenirs of my past relieved me of my grief and despair. There were also days when sleep wouldn't come and, with nothing else to do, I sat and mulled over my memories. I imagined Sarah's soft breathing while she slept, and the wind chimes on the dogwood in our yard. I yearned for her laughter and for our idle talk. I missed her humming along with the music of Billie Holiday.

"In my medieval history class, yesterday," she

announced, while pouring coffee one morning, "I asked one of the boys to give me a characteristic of the Middle Ages."

"And?"

"He said: 'Menopause! Right, Mrs. Gilman?'"

I laughed.

"Don't laugh. It's not funny."

"Actually, it's very funny. What did you do?"

"I kicked him out," she said remorsefully. "He was just being a smart ass to impress the girls. I'm such a prude."

"He'll get over it. It's a badge of honor now. They're probably telling the story in the halls right now."

"I got old on you, mister. My own students are mocking me with menopause jokes. And they don't even know that was five years ago."

I understood why she was telling me the story. "Hey, take a look over here," I pointed to my wrinkled forehead, gray stubble, and sagging chin.

This was clearly no help.

"You're not twenty anymore," I said, "but you still look like the girl on the train to me. You always will."

She smiled. "'Do you have any motza?' What were you thinking?"

Emunah's *volunteers* arrived almost daily, hell-bent on introducing me to all the activities I was missing while grieving in my room. "Bingo and wheelchair exercise are very, very popular," one woman lectured me as we toured the facility. "And arts and crafts — the painting class in particular — are actually rejuvenating. It's extremely important to stay upbeat you know."

I loathed their visits, but the excursions usually ended

in the dining room, and it was there that I was indoctrinated into my new surroundings. The staff — who I sat beside to avoid the other patients — referred to us clinically, as "beds" (they described beds opening up when someone died; the new thirty-bed Acute Disability Facility, and my peers were characterized with linen references: "301B, man, that pillow has lost its feathers"). And my floormates, who spoke too loudly and without concern for anyone nearby, discussed their various medical conditions openly and graphically; moving one's bowels and urinating, for example, being some kind of litmus tests for survival.

"Lima beans? Again? There's not enough gas around here as it is?"

"It's not the beans. It's the mushy bananas."

"The mushy what? Eh, forget it. I have to pee; empty the old *sockledodger*."

"A sockledodger's a big one. You — you got a *pintel*."

"What should we do today?" a young aide asked me one afternoon, perhaps six weeks into my stay. "How about a walk around the grounds?" She paused for my reply, but got none. "Would you like me to help you get a coat?"

"No. I need my privacy today — Please."

She moved behind my wheelchair. "Why don't we take a little trip out to the porch. Everyone loves it out there."

"That's not a word," I said to Sarah one summer during a Scrabble game on our patio. "Qanat? You made that up."

"Challenge it. Here's the dictionary. Thirty-seven points and you'll lose your turn, but go ahead. Q-A-N-A-T. Yep, that's right."

"First, you forgot the "u" after the "q." Second, that's not a word," I repeated. "But if you

want to lose, hand me the dictionary."

Too quickly it was in my hand.

***Qanat** n. : Underground tunnel*

"When did that word come up in conversation?"

"Gloating rights. It's worth it to know."

"I'm not up to meeting anyone today," I said, as the memory faded.

She moved around to face me, put her hands on the armrests and bent over me. "You need some companionship." She took my hand in hers. "Everyone said you and your wife were the cutest couple; that you're such a sweet man. She wouldn't want you to close yourself off, you know."

"Please," I said. "Perhaps tomorrow."

There was a long pause as she dropped down heavily on the bed. "Ten minutes? Then you can wheel yourself back. The porch is nice. You might like it."

Porch, to me, meant a pleasant area bordering a backyard furnished with chaise lounges, wicker chairs, and picnic tables. In contrast, the porch at Emunah was little more than a large airy den providing the residents with a place to gather. The walls were painted pastel pinks and yellows, giving the room a sunny quality, almost reminiscent of springtime, and this atmosphere was augmented by rows of chives and basil growing in window boxes, and leafy flowers hanging in macramé webs from the ceiling.

"Look at this tomato plant," Sarah said to me one afternoon. "Six feet tall and one lousy tomato. How is that possible?"

"I have no idea."

"I wanted to be like one of those little old ladies who calls to all her neighbors, in her house-coat, and offers baskets of ripe tomatoes."

"Seems like a problem," I said, not knowing whether to agree or be falsely encouraging.

"Mrs. Green," Sarah called to a phantom streetmate in a poor Italian accent. "Come over here, I have a beautiful wedge of tomato for you. Come. Come. You can make a teaspoon of sauce."

I scanned the porch. I was struck by a sense that something was missing. My expectation was to see staff in great numbers and volunteers working diligently with each resident, exactly as Brody, and indeed all the literature, had pledged. To my surprise, the only visible personnel were those who sat chatting at the nurses' station just outside the porch and across the hall, one of whom nodded to me.

"Are you deaf?" a small hunched man said to me. He had risen from his chair and caned his way toward me.

"Can you hear me?" he shouted, as everyone turned to look at us. "You don't talk at lunch when you're there. Why not?"

"I can hear you. Thank you."

"Sit down, Maury." The order came from a woman — Mrs. Goodman, I would later learn — at a small table near the doorway who, though she was sitting, gripped the walker next to her with a tight fist. A glance around the room told me my annoyance was not unique.

He shrugged and shuffled back to his chair, muttering, and I continued my survey. Aside from yarn work, TV, and cards, the list of activities on the porch was short — remarkably short and undeniably uninspired. There were readers, a good number, dispersed around the more well-lit areas, with books piled at their feet, and there was one man who seemed busy with what appeared to be a terrarium, or perhaps an ant farm, perched on a stand near the television. It was all so dreary.

I went back to my room a short while later and thought about what I had seen. The monotony is planned, I thought. The absence of exuberance made it safe. Everyone here is sheltered from becoming overwrought, and made calm and indifferent to what some social scientist might have deemed dangerous and debilitating passions.

For a moment, I considered confronting Brody on this planned inactivity. In my mind, at our imaginary meeting, I called him a liar and threatened to contact the social services agency to complain on behalf of the group.

The thought passed. Who was I, after all, to make a fuss?

I was struck, then, by the revelation that I confused them; the intensity of my grief must have had them worried. I wondered, also, how many others there mourned in secret; how many people on the porch had as much disdain for their fates as I did mine.

"I have cancer."
Sarah's words made me shudder.
"We'll get through it," I said.
"No. This time, I'm afraid we won't."

FEBRUARY 1948

Elie Wasserman entered Hecht House, his gym clothes in a burlap sack thrown across his back. He studied the basketball court and could see Hy Rifkin near the locker room door screaming at Joel Mochiber, who was struggling with his shoelaces.

Hecht House reminded Elie of Hy. Both Hy and Hecht House arrived into the world during the late 1880s, and neither had aged well at all. Hy was cross to nearly everyone, and the building groaned with every wind. Both also seemed gray and worn to Elie. Hy had thick, charcoal eyebrows always slanted in an angry glare. The gym was dim and shabby. Hy had run Hecht House for forty years.

Elie studied the chipping Star of David painted on the wall behind one basket. He thought about his first experience with Hy several years earlier. "They'll come for us again, the bastards," Hy declared after the German's had surrendered. "Next time we'll be ready!" Elie was fourteen then and had little time for sports between school and his job at Isaac Gurlock's Hardware Store. His teammates had even less. Most had spent the majority of their time learning the Talmud and few had even seen a basketball.

Hy's shouting in the distance reminded Elie of the team's first practice. The boys from the different synagogues had eyed one another as if they were certain the others were infected with the plague. The Hassidic boys from Khal Anshei Chessed and Adas Yeraim, wore black coats, tzitzits, and wide-brimmed hats. Those who were Orthodox and still tended to ritual, came from Congregation Sfath Emes but had shed the more traditional dress for shorts and undershirts purchased by the congregation. In stark contrast, the boys from Ohab Zedek and B'nai Zion had no mandated clothing nor gifts of uniforms.

"We have to break them down, before we can build them up," Hy said to one parent that first day. "Loyalty to one another is earned, not taught." Elie realized early on that Hy's coaching method was built on insults and taunting.

"You're letting that little Hassid Joel beat you. Ech, you'll be the laughingstock of Ohab Zedek," Hy screamed at Elie during one practice when it was synagogue versus synagogue. "Rip his pitiful tzitzit off if you have to. You think God will care he doesn't wear his worthless fringes. Don't let that little bookworm get near the ball."

Elie ran to the locker room to change, punching Joel's arm playfully, and winking at Hy to annoy him.

"We want to play other teams in the city," Elie said nervously to Hy at the onset of practices their second year.

"They'll rip you apart," Hy told him. "You're just a bunch of sissy Talmud readers. You read all day and hold your mother's aprons all night. They're tough. Even their sisters could kill you."

"We aren't afraid," Elie replied. "You might be, but we're not."

Elie remembered that they had taken the name "Zionists" even though it created a stir. Most Hassidic Jews believed Zionism and Judaism were diametrically opposed and vehemently objected. "Politics cannot do what God has not yet done," Rabbi Liebenshul from Khal Anshei Chessed declared. "The name is blasphemous." Elie knew

Rabbi Liebenshul's congregation had come from Russia after the pogroms of 1900, and he understood that neither their devotion nor their practices had changed in two centuries. "Only God can create Israel. Children should not hear such a word."

Rabbi Kishenev from Adas Yeraim had spoken to his colleague. Elie did not know what was said, but the team took the name.

"They need two tables and ten chairs," Elie heard Hy shouting at someone. "It's the Library Exchange. A table of old books and ratty magazines. I will set them up in the far corner. Such *tsourus* over nothing." Elie knew Hy tried not to offend anyone who had a use for the gym. "They like to kibbitz about who's gonna be the mayor or what's gonna happen in Israel. Who am I to say they can't have it?"

Joel came in. "They're out there. They're huge. By the way, what's a tam-o'-shanter?"

"I think it's a hat," Elie said. He pulled on socks. "They were big last year too, and only beat us by thirty so don't worry about it. Besides, I am guessing they're looking at you a bit wide-eyed." Joel had grown almost six inches in the last year and now towered above his teammates.

The game went well at first, but the superior size and speed of the Tam-o'-Shanters began to wear down the Zionists. At the end of the first half Hecht House was down by twelve points.

Hy huddled the Zionists underneath their basket during halftime. "Ech, total embarrassment. What, you like total embarrassment? I hope you like it. You see those Mick bastards over there," he pointed at the Tam-o'-Shanters. "They are laughing at you. This is easy for them. Yudie, you should go home. Go study. What you know in your head may be the only thing these potato boys can't steal from you."

"We were nervous, Hy," Elie interrupted, "a lot of people are here watching."

Hy glared at Elie. "You think this is like stickball? Do you think that? These people would just as soon see you dead, as they would beat you. You have learned nothing? When these Nazi sympathizers beat you, you're one step closer to the ovens and the showers. Do you understand this? These people are your enemies. These people see you walking down the street and they think to themselves: I am better than that Jew. I hate that Jew."

"They're Irish, aren't they?" one of the boys asked. "What are you talking about?"

"It makes no difference who they are or where they come from. In the end, they would have been willing to shoot you and your family like dogs in the street."

"Hy," Elie said, "just tell us how to play defense against them. My legs are so tired from chasing them, I think they must have extra men out there."

"You want to play defense against them? Hate them more than they hate you. Hate them so much that your blood boils and pushes your legs like pistons. Then you will never get tired. If they push you, you push them back harder. If they laugh at you, you tell those criminals you'll see them in Hell. Make your hate give you strength. That works for them. They are tossing you aside like water thrown from a pail."

Hy walked away.

"I have known Whitey Cleary since I was five," Yudie said to Elie. "I wouldn't say we were close friends, but hate him? I don't hate him. I'm sorry."

"They don't look like they're laughing, either," another boy added. He wiped his forehead with his shirt. "They look worried. I think Joel makes them nervous."

"Joel makes me nervous too," Yudie said. "He fell on me last year. I almost died."

The game continued, and suddenly Joel was everywhere, blocking shots and lofting the ball to his teammates for easy baskets. Elie realized it was the Tam-o'-Shanters who now were puzzled. He stole the ball once and scored, as did Yudie, and the game was close. The Tam-o'-Shanters screamed at one another to do something, but Elie realized none of them knew what to do. Elie could see Hy was almost overcome with excitement. With one minute to play, the Tam-o'-Shanters led by only one.

A time out was taken when the Library Exchange ended, and a line of women filed under the Zionists' basket carrying stacks of books. The Zionists would get the ball, and Elie knew that this was to be their last chance to win.

The teams took the court and the ball was thrown to Yudie, who held it for several seconds. Yudie passed to Elie who dribbled slowly on the floor, eyeing the man defending him. "Ten," said the referee. Without looking, Elie lofted a pass underneath the basket where Joel waited, concentrating on the ball. Joel grabbed the pass in both hands with his back to the basket and in a single movement turned to take the shot.

Elie watched Whitey Cleary try to play defense against Joel. Whitey had tried in vain to stay between Joel and any pass that might come, and now that Joel had the ball, Elie realized, suddenly, there was no one between his massive teammate and the basket.

"Shoot!" Elie screamed.

But before he could, Elie watched in desperation as Whitey swiped, and plucked the only thing he could see to grab, Joel's black skullcap.

Elie looked on in panic. Joel was preparing to jump when he felt the bobby pins twist and the cap fly from his head. His knees were coiled to spring, and his hands and arms were extending toward the basket when Whitey's reckless defense took hold. Joel dropped the ball and felt the back of his head with both hands. "Oh my God. If Rabbi Kishenev hears of this —" he said aloud. "Or if God sees this —"

From where he stood, Elie watched the events unfold. After throwing the pass to Joel, instinct told him to move back — to play defense — and his legs followed without any thought. As the ball came loose, for a moment his body urged him to run forward, to try to push aside the others, and score. Before he could move, however, he saw Whitey grab the ball, and as the referee continued the count — "five, four" — heave it as far from the basket as he could.

Elie caught Whitey's heave at mid-court and heard the referee shout "two" as the ball settled in his hands. With one motion, he launched the ball toward the basket. As the ball left his outstretched arms, he uttered the only words that came into his head: "Please, God."

He knew immediately that the shot was not straight. It would travel the needed distance, he saw, but it was far to the left of where it should be. From the corner of his eye he saw Joel kiss his yarmulke and then hold it to the top of his head. He noticed, too, the others on the court gazing with either hope or dread at the flight of his shot. As the ball started down, he also realized, a young woman was passing beneath the basket, book in hand.

Had no one shouted, the ball might have merely grazed Dina Kishenev's head. She had minutes earlier borrowed *The Sun Also Rises* from the Exchange, and her head was down as she read and walked. That a game raged on the court near her was irrelevant.

"Look out, Dina!" Yudie screamed.

Dina stopped and looked upward. The ball crashed squarely into her face.

The referee blew his whistle signaling that the game

was over. The Zionists gathered around Dina Kishenev who lay still on the gym floor with her eyes closed and her head in Yudie's lap. Her nose was bleeding. In the background, the Tam-o'-Shanters celebrated their victory.

"Elie, she's not dead, is she?" Joel asked.

"She'll be fine," Yudie interrupted. "Elie, you, I am not so sure about."

"It's just a game," one of the boys scolded Yudie. "Besides, it wasn't Elie's fault. The shot was from fifty feet away."

"That's not what I'm talking about," Yudie said.

Hy approached the circle around Dina and leaned over Yudie's shoulder. "Oye, the rabbi's daughter. You couldn't hit Fishbein's daughter? She's got a nose like her father's anyway." He turned and walked away. "Rabbi Kishenev'll have my head," he muttered as he went.

"This is the rabbi's daughter?" Elie asked.

"Wow, she's beautiful," Joel said.

"How do you know she's beautiful, you moron? There's blood all over her," Yudie said.

"With my eyes, I can see," Joel argued. "I've seen her before at the Franklin Field Wall on Rosh Hashana."

Dina coughed and raised a hand to her face where a red-streaked handkerchief covered her nose.

"Please tell your father I tried to help you," Yudie continued. "There's your killer." He pointed to Elie. "I'm just here to rescue Your Ladyship. And to warn my friends not to get too close to you. Getting smashed in the face with cold shoulders is much worse than any basketball."

"Yudie, a little sympathy might be more effective. I better take you home," Elie said, leaning down to her. "Can you sit for one minute while I get my clothes?" Dina nodded.

"Has a rabbi ever killed anyone?" Yudie asked.

"Don't say things like that," Joel protested.

"A little joke," Yudie said. "So, shoot me."

Elie ran into the dim locker room and gathered his belongings. He worried that he couldn't explain to Rabbi Kishenev how such an accident could happen. "*You couldn't see my beautiful daughter standing there?*" He worried, also, that Yudie might be right, that this girl could be unforgiving. Also, later that night, he'd have to describe the events of the evening to his own mother. He imagined the worry in her face.

Yudie and Joel had moved Dina to a chair and they sat around her in silence. When he ran to her, Elie could see that her face was swollen, and he wished, fervently, that he had not let go of the shot that had struck her. The chance of success had been slim, perhaps non-existent, and now he had the loss and disastrous results to explain.

"Can you walk?" Elie asked, kneeling in front of Dina.

"All over you," Yudie responded. "Just ask poor Bernard, the Chosen."

"Yudie!" Elie said. "It's not bad enough?"

"Cynicism is my best thing, Elie. You know that. Don't act so surprised." He looked around at his friends. "I just hate to lose to those guys. It's just too much for me." He paused. "Sorry. Do you know where she lives?"

"No," Elie acknowledged.

"Behind Adas Yeraim. The door is on the Wilmore Street side, at the back of the synagogue. You'll see it."

The other boys moved toward the shower room and left Elie alone with Dina. "I'm so sorry," Elie said, crouching in front of her. "Would it make you feel better to know that I don't think Yudie should talk to you the way he does? I'm sorry for that too."

"I understand," she sniffled. "You don't like my father, do you? That's it, isn't it? This was an attempt at sabotage." She opened one eye and looked at Elie's clothing. He had put on a sweater and old corduroys. "You must be from B'nai Zion. I'm going to call the police. The police might even help a Jewish girl if there was an injury. They don't like to get involved in disputes between synagogues, though. You knew that when you threw the ball. Didn't you?"

Elie was captivated by her look and her downy voice. Still, he wanted to tease her for her dramatics. He thought better of it. "Honest, I didn't try to hit you. I was taking a shot. I missed."

"You did not miss! You hit me right in the face. I didn't know basketball was so dangerous. I've decided never to let my children play such a game."

"It isn't usually so dangerous. You were just walking in the wrong place."

"I — I was walking in the wrong place!" She pushed him with her foot, and he tumbled from his crouch onto the floor. "Oh, you should be ashamed of yourself. First you try to deliberately maim me — to get back at Bernard, I'm sure, no matter where you pray — then you have the insensitivity to blame me for my own injuries. You'll be lucky if my father doesn't exile you from the city. And if he doesn't do that, my brother will, when he's ordained in a few years. I'll ask him to, and he will. He does whatever I say."

Elie glanced around the nearly empty gym. "People don't get put out of Mattapan." He liked her.

"I know that," she said. "I didn't know whether you did, though." She got up. "Bernard has probably already heard of this disaster. He'll be here in a minute to take me home. You can leave now if you want."

"I am going to take you home. You don't look very steady, and Hy will lock the gym with you inside if it is time to close up and this Bernard is not here. It is one of Hy's idiosyncrasies." Elie picked up her book. "Besides, I think I better explain to your mother and father what happened. Nothing's gone right so far tonight and, if you tell them, I just might be exiled. I can see Goldberg's newsletter next week: Wasserman loses game, injures rabbi's daughter, and becomes the first exile in American history. All in one night."

Dina smiled, but caught herself. "If you think I should feel sorry for you, I don't. In fact, after you tell my parents how your aim left me with these permanent scars, I think you should go tell Rebbe Liebenshul, also."

She held Elie's arm, and they moved through the gym and out to the street. "Are you all right?" he asked, after they had walked a few more steps. She didn't answer.

Without speaking, they walked for several blocks. As they crossed onto Blue Hill Avenue, Elie watched her try to locate a nearby curb. Joel was correct, he decided, as he helped her. She was beautiful. Her eyes were hazel and glistened even in the dim light. Her brown hair fell over one eye and swept across her neck, and her skin was milky and smelled of rosewater. Even through the swelling, he could see she had delicate features accentuated by dimples on both cheeks.

"You're that boy that the churches wouldn't give the writing prize to, aren't you?" she said, studying him.

He shrugged. "It was a stupid idea."

"I didn't think so."

"My father wrote for a newspaper. Before he — Anyway, I'd like to be a journalist someday too; so I thought it might be good practice."

"Your father passed away?"

Elie didn't feel like answering. He didn't know what to say anyway. *He's been missing since the war. My mother is too afraid to let me make inquiries about him; she knows he was probably killed and can't face it.* The subject made him queasy and distraught.

Dina did not press him.

"This Bernard, he's going to be a rabbi?" Elie asked.

"He will be the Rebbe of Khal Anshei Chessed," Dina said. "And then my father says that after we're married, someday all the congregations will be joined together. My father is very worried about the way the congregations have grown apart. He says everyone is suspicious of everyone else." Elie saw her study him; she clearly wanted to see whether he believed her. He didn't. She caught herself and pretended to ignore him.

She's not really mad, he thought. This girl fascinates me.

"The people at B'nai Zion and Ohab Zedek, he says, try to blend in with the rest of the city to protect themselves by disappearing into the crowd. And Rebbe Liebenshul, and Bernard, they hold on to tradition so tightly, Papa says, it's as if they were afraid someone could take it from them. Everyone has reacted to the camps, Father says, and that is why he's worked hard to continue as if nothing had ever happened in Europe. He says we can't let a madman affect the way we worship our God. You can't pray, he says, with one eye on the door, waiting for it to be broken down." She moved her hair away from her face. "Papa says it's difficult at times to communicate with the other congregations because of what's happened. It makes him very sad sometimes."

"I'm not very good at praying," Elie remarked, remembering his plea to God just before the final shot. "I don't think that I know Bernard. Is he nice?"

"He is going to be the Rebbe of Khal Amnshei Chessed, so of course he's nice. If you mean, does he play basketball? No, he doesn't have time to waste on things like that. If you're preparing to be a rabbi, you spend almost all your time in school, studying Talmud. My father did and well —" She frowned. Elie could see that she was in pain. "Why would you imply that Bernard wasn't nice.

I'll tell you, your friend Yudie Kosasky isn't nice. I don't know why he's so mean to me."

"Yudie is mean to everyone," Elie said. "That is just the way Yudie is. To be honest, I think he might like you more than you think. Anyway, I didn't mean to imply anything about Bernard. I don't know him. I just assumed that since you've decided to marry him that you must think he's nice."

"He's nice," Dina replied flatly.

Elie realized he was glad to be with her. It made him lighthearted and animated.

They had reached Adas Yeraim, and in the dim light of the street lamps, Elie examined the structure. The building was large and windowless. It was built of red bricks, discolored by years of wear. Though Elie had passed by the synagogue many times before, until that evening he had never wondered what took place behind the huge oaken doorway; the entrance to the sanctuary. They walked to the back of the building. This was her home as well.

Dina opened the door and stepped into the darkened foyer. Two children, a boy and a girl, jumped almost at once into her arms. "Are you dead?" one of them, a little girl, asked. "Mrs. Shetzel rung Mama and said you had an accident," the other said, grabbing Dina's face with two hands to examine her injuries. "Your nose looks funny," he said. Elie guessed the children were twins.

The first child looked at Elie who was still on the step outside. "You're not Bernard," she announced. "Dina," she whispered loudly in her sister's ear, "someone's here."

Elie heard footsteps approaching the foyer. Dina lowered the children to the floor.

Dina's mother switched on a light in the foyer. "Are you all right?" she asked. "Mrs. Shetzel told me, just now, that such a terrible thing happened at the Library Exchange." She examined her child under the lightbulb. "Eh, it's not such a terrible thing. A little knock on the *keppele*. You'll live. Your nose is a little swollen, that's all. Oye, Mrs. Shetzel made such a fuss."

"Mama," Dina protested. She gestured at Elie, who was still outside. "He threw a ball at me. It hit me in the face." Her mother smiled. "He was attempting to deliberately hurt me. I was bleeding, and I crumpled to the floor in a heap. People thought I was dead. Everyone crowded around me, and I was nearly unconscious the pain was so terrible. I'm surprised I was able to walk home."

"I think you'll be all right," Mrs. Kishenev said, amused.

"I'm not so sure. I'm feeling a little dizzy, even now. You just can't imagine the aching. When he hit me, the whole world spun around. I felt like I was falling into a bottomless pit, and then the next thing I'm on the floor, with every inch of my body in agony. It was like a thousand daggers were stabbing me or people were beating me on the head with sticks." She glanced at Elie. "And it was even more painful to watch him aim carefully, then throw with all of his strength directly at me."

Mrs. Kishenev turned to look at Elie. "That *punum*? I think your senses may have been knocked loose, that's all."

Elie laughed. The mother and daughter were alike, and he enjoyed them both.

"I was on the floor, the room was spinning around. Yudie Kosasky was saying terrible things about me while I was trying to regain consciousness. He's such an awful boy. And do you know, Mother, the only thing I could think about while I was in such horrible agony was, of course, my wonderful Bernard. I thought, if only Bernard were here, he would swoop in and lift me off of the floor. He would have carried me home, while I lay limp in his arms from my injuries, my head thrown back over his shoulder. All the way home he would have whispered sweet, reassuring words in my ear. And when he got here he would have set me down on my bed, kissed me gently on the lips, and then sat by my bedside until I was well again."

"Bernard never lifted anything heavier than a prayer book his whole life."

Elie stifled another grin. Dina was mad.

"This is the truth, and you know it," Mrs. Kishenev insisted. "Now, inside and hold a cold cloth on that forehead. Do it now, or you'll look like Sylvia Fishbein, God forbid." She waved at Elie to approach. "You should have a cup of tea before you go. Come inside. Come."

Elie stepped into the kitchen and noticed the two children he had seen earlier kneeling on chairs at a table in the center of the room. They had wooden bowls in front of them and long wooden spoons in their hands. Their faces were spattered with batter. "Are you Bernard?" the little boy asked. Bernard looks different from you."

"No," Elie said gently, "my name is Elie. What are your names?"

"My name is Reyna," the girl replied, "and my brother's name is Judah Kishenev."

"I could have told it," Judah protested, his mouth overflowing.

"And what is your last name?" Mrs. Kishenev asked. "Do I think I know you?"

"Wasserman."

"I know your mother. Not well, but I know her, I think. Your father was lost during the war. Is that right?"

"Yes, that's right." Elie wondered how she knew about his family, but was distracted by the children. He made a face at them, and they giggled. "I am sorry I hit Dina. I didn't mean to. I was aiming at the basket."

"Your aim's not so good," Mrs. Kishenev chided him.

"But I know this wasn't intentional. If it had been, Mrs. Shetzel would have been hysterical. As it was, she was just excited to be the first to tell me."

Dina returned to the kitchen, pressing a cloth against her nose and eyes. Her shiny brown hair fell loosely about her shoulders. Another boy followed Dina into the kitchen. Elie guessed he was about eleven. "You sure gave my sister some shiners," he said. "Thanks. Somebody should have clocked her a long time ago."

"Mrs. Liebenshul would not allow such talk," Dina declared.

"Mrs. Liebenshul has only Bernard, who has no sisters," her mother said. "If she had daughters, there would be such talk. This, I can promise you."

"But —"

"Hush, our guest will think the Rebbe of Adas Yeraim has a family that only whines."

The kettle began to boil just as the rabbi entered the kitchen. He was a round man with an attentive expression. He removed his talises, and kissed the two youngsters. "Your son is going to be a fine rabbi," he said to his wife. "He told Mrs. Shiffman, this afternoon, that the Talmud commands that all mourning is to end with the placing of the headstone. She only carried on for three hours today, not seven. So, what's the harm. A good, small lie." He shrugged. "Dina, your beautiful face," he said, staring. "You look like Sylvia Fishbein. May God forgive me for saying such things."

"Rabbi!" Mrs. Kishenev said.

"Papa, I was just minding my own business at the Exchange, when I was assaulted. I can't think of any other family who would invite someone for tea who did such a thing. Bernard's family would have him exiled."

"What is this with exiled this week?" The rabbi said to his wife. "Are you reading about Napoleon?" His wife did not answer. She put a teapot and several cups on the table.

"You don't look so dangerous," the Rabbi said to Elie.

"It was a basketball, but it was an accident, Rabbi, honest," Elie pleaded. "I wouldn't hurt anyone on purpose. But I probably shouldn't have taken the shot anyway. I was too far away. It just happened."

"He told me I shouldn't have been walking under the basket while the game was on."

"And who is he? Might I ask such a question?"

"His name is Elie," Reyna said. "He just told me."

"This is Elie Wasserman, dear," Mrs. Kishenev said. "You know his mother, Lena Wasserman. Her husband isn't —"

"I'm sorry, your mother, I don't think I know." He raised his shoulders and put his hands up to ask for forgiveness. "What shul do you attend? Perhaps that will help me with a face."

"Ohab Zedek. But that's okay, my mother's very quiet. You probably wouldn't know her."

Mrs. Kishenev appeared exasperated at her husband. "I can't say I know her if I don't know her," he defended himself.

"You know her. You know everyone. You're just getting old and forgetful, that's all."

"Papa, did you telephone Rabbi Liebenshul?" Dina said.

"Was I supposed to telephone the rebbe?" he asked his wife.

"Someone should call him and tell him I've been severely disfigured. I obviously can't tell him." Dina closed her eyes. "You can tell him also that I'll understand if he no longer finds me suitable to marry his son. I can just go and work with the Red Cross; tend to the sick and injured the rest of my life, lonely and in despair."

Reyna giggled. "You're so funny," she said.

"Whose child is this?" the rabbi asked his wife. "No one from my side of the family knows from such dramatics. Wasn't your Uncle Max in the theater? You see what happens with such influences. Where else could she get such ideas?"

"My Uncle Max has been dead thirty years," Mrs. Kishenev declared, picking up Elie's empty teacup. "There is only one person in this family on stage regularly and that's you."

"I better be going," Elie said. "My mother will wonder where I am. Thank you very much for the tea. I hope you'll be okay, Dina. I'm sorry. Honest."

"Just tell me one thing," the rabbi asked. "My friend Hy, he's all right?"

"He's fine, Rabbi. He's taking good care of the gym."

"All right, tell me one more thing. Did you win the game? Please God. Did we show Father McTiernan Joel Mochiber, and did they run away in fear?"

"We lost by one point. But Joel made them very nervous."

"Well, nervous is good," the Rabbi said. "Next game we'll win."

"I hope so," Elie reflected for a moment on Whitey Cleary's devious tactic. He thanked Mrs. Kishenev again, then walked out into the night air. He could see Reyna and Judah watching him from the door.

He passed the Norfolk Street Playground. A full moon gleamed above the treetops, and the air was cool and moist against his face. He stopped for a moment to consider the night, and his prayer earlier that evening came again into his head, "Please God," he repeated to himself. For a moment he wished he had been more specific; "Please God let it go in the basket," he decided might have been more appropriate. "So, I'm sorry," Elie called, looking up to the heavens. "I should have been more clear. Would it have been so hard though, to figure it out for yourself? Oh, that's okay."

After a few steps Dina returned to his thoughts.

MAY 1991

To avoid the overbearing volunteers, I wheeled myself to the porch the next morning, toting a book on my lap to foster the idea that conversations should be carried on elsewhere, somewhere away from me.

"Abe, do you know Rose Goodman?" an orderly asked, indicating the woman with the walker sitting next to me, as I situated my chair.

Rose turned to me. "I understand you're mourning for your wife. The Talmud allows this to go on as long as necessary. Be careful, however, not to let grief swarm over you."

> *"I'm so sorry for your loss," Sarah said to my eighty-three-year-old Uncle Rueben, whose best friend had passed away. We were at the reception following the funeral.*
>
> *"He was in our poker group," Reuben responded, swathed in dejection. "Bill, Jack, Larry, Ed and I, twice a month."*
>
> *Sarah peered at him quizzically. Except for my uncle, they were all dead.*
>
> *"I hope you learn to play solitaire," she said.*

Rose turned her attention to the nurses. "Belinda,

Maury will need tea now and Mrs. Cohen needs more light. There's not enough light for her there."

"A minute," Belinda, the head nurse called from outside the door. "I'm just making the tea." She was a round woman with an ever-present optimistic grin that I, for some inexplicable reason, thought was perfectly consistent with her shock of orange hair and her freckles.

"Hannah, are you all right for a moment?" Belinda shouted. I saw several heads turn toward a woman sitting near the far windows. The woman had a book in her lap and appeared to be captivated. People who loved to read seemed always to appear entranced, and I had once desperately wanted to have readers lost in settings and characters I had created. I wanted nothing more than to walk down the beach in summer and see people sunning themselves while reading a book I had authored, each of my readers wearing an expression exactly as Hannah Cohen wore now.

"Hannah?" Belinda repeated.

Hannah Cohen seemed startled for a moment, almost as if she was unsure whether the voice calling to her was real or from somewhere within the pages in which she was immersed.

"Thank you," she finally responded with a pleasant smile. Hannah had a particularly easy expression and soft, well-preserved features. She, in fact, did not look as if she belonged with the others; she seemed more alert. The wheelchair, which I could see beneath the blanket, looked out of place. "There is no hurry, Belinda. My eyes need to rest for a moment, anyway. Whenever you get to it will be fine."

"I'll be there in a minute," Belinda offered, sticking her head inside the door. "I have some news for everyone, anyway." She was out of sight again, apparently back at her station.

"What, a cup of tea is so hard to make?" Maury declared loudly, startling nearly everyone. "A little Lipton bag in boiling water, that's all. Is that so hard?" Maury glanced around for reassurance that he was within his rights to complain. "What's so hard, right? And put sugar in it today," he groused. "Every day I ask for sugar. Do I ever get any sugar? No, of course not. It's only Maury asking. Why should I get any sugar?" Exasperated at the complaining, I felt both worn and beleaguered.

"Eh, you're a Goddamn diabetic, you Goddamn son of a bitch. They ain't gonna give you sugar. Now shut up." The voice came from the card table across the room, where one of the players was gathering up the pot. An uneven babble of disagreement at the table briefly overwhelmed the conversation.

"Listen to me, you old bastard," the man continued. "Every day, every day you ask for sugar. Never once has she brought you sugar. Stop asking for fucking sugar." Maury's tormentor was small and full of frowns, and his white hair was disheveled and oily. The bones in his face appeared to loosen as he spoke.

"Harry, leave him be," Belinda said handing a mug to Maury. "I'll tell him when to stop asking."

Harry turned further in his seat until he was sitting sideways. He grinned at Maury. "Eh, all right, all right. Hey, you old bastard," he said to Maury, "did you hear about the guy who goes into the Army/Navy store and asks if they got any camouflage pants?"

"No," Maury replied. He seemed to appreciate the attention.

"The clerk says, yeah, but we can't fuckin' find 'em." He coughed violently as he laughed. "That Goddamn joke reminds me of you." He gasped and coughed again. "I can't fucking find 'em," he repeated softly to himself as he returned his focus to the game. "Shuffle the Goddamn cards," he ordered, "it's three hours between hands with you *chuzzeri.*"

"Such a deal to get any tea at all," Maury said ignoring Harry's insult. "You say it's okay. It must be okay. I'm not one to complain." He lifted the mug, sipped the tea and grimaced. "Very nice. Such a deal."

> *"Two teachers! What a deal," the principal of a school Sarah and I taught at early in our careers said at our interview. "Is it a deal breaker if you don't get the classes you want? No? Good deal! Such a deal that you came when you did. We needed good teachers. No big deal of course but"*
>
> *"What an or-deal," Sarah whispered.*

I opened my book, but could only scan the pages.

My leg began to ache and I closed the book to rub my thigh. My skin still seemed numb, almost paper-thin, but though the area was deadened, when I pressed on the bone an icy sensation ran up my spine. The feeling was not pleasant, but was at least a consequence on which I could rely. When I considered that I could still barely move my toes, I was grateful to have any reactive response at all.

"Mr. Gilman, do you need help?" Belinda called. "Abe?"

I stared at her, stunned that she had been watching me and exhaled to augment my expression of defeat. I desperately wanted to tell her that I did not want to be bothered or even noticed, but I just as badly wanted her to understand me without having to explain myself publicly.

"Can I get you something," Belinda asked. She had approached me, and placed a hand on my shoulder. "A blanket?"

"I'm not cold," I said, "My leg hurts . . . No, nothing. Please, not now."

She put up her hand. "Sorry, I'll try not to bother you." I had clearly hurt her feelings

"Listen for one moment everyone, please," she called from behind me. She smoothed her uniform as she spoke. "As I told you, I have some news."

I looked over to Hannah Cohen to see if she found it necessary to listen. I figured if this apparent island in the sea of insanity into which I had sailed deemed the announcement noteworthy, I would follow her lead. If she ignored Belinda, then I would follow suit. I rubbed the open pages in my lap, ready to continue, but I found that Hannah Cohen had closed her own book and was listening carefully, an expression on her face of genuine interest and sympathy.

"We will have another new face around here beginning this afternoon," Belinda announced. "His name is Samuel Levine Hersh. Some of you may know him. Anyone? No one?"

Someone near me groaned. "I hope," Belinda said, reacting to the response, "he'll be given a very warm welcome."

I wondered whether my arrival had been similarly announced, and concluded that it was. I was equally sure the reaction was the same, though I thought that the reluctance to embrace Hersh may have been my doing. My unfriendliness must have been dispiriting during the past weeks. I shrugged and focused again on Hannah Cohen.

"So, you're a widower," Gertie Neustadt, said, approaching me. Unnerved, I said nothing.

"That happens," she continued, her voice raspy and harsh. "People come, they go. Only God can choose." I looked back to Hannah, who had returned to her book. "We have all heard about your wife and how lovely and nice she was; funny, they say. You should give thanks for such a blessing."

Weariness swept over me, though it was not physical fatigue, but rather the exhaustion of my faculties. My head felt as if it were full of thick syrup; my thoughts, dulled by what felt like saturation, and the heaviness of physical discomfit. A room full of strangers, widowed, crippled, unable to concentrate or even read. I had no idea at all why I was even alive.

"Please," I said, "please, I just need to be — I have a bit of a headache. I think I'd like to just sit quietly for a moment. Would that be all right?"

She looked around the room, and I realized, was about to call for Belinda.

"No, no," I begged her. "I'll be fine. I just need to rest my eyes quietly for a minute. We can talk again later."

"So, all right, I'll go," she said, getting the gist. "I'll go." She adjusted her shawl and moved away.

"Christ, all right, all right," I heard Harry proclaim. "He likes to Goddamn read, not play cards. Why do I always — all right —" I looked up. Belinda was crouched next to Harry's chair, motioning to me. "Play any Goddamn cards?" he asked, without enthusiasm.

"No," I said flatly. Belinda urged Harry on by tapping his knee.

"Shit," he spit out. "Nothing? Poker? Canasta? Hearts, Goddammit?" He turned back to Belinda, who nodded for him to continue. "The guy doesn't play. He doesn't play. Okay already?"

"Let him be, dear," Rose Goodman ordered firmly. "If Mr. Gilman wants to join the game — *halavai.*"

There was a hierarchy on the porch, I realized. As a result of my reputation and my ill moods, I was sure I would occupy the lowest rung, even though others with their doddering eccentricities appeared, in my mind at least, to be more deserving of such a fate. Harry, on the other hand, occupied a spot near the top of the heap, a position he had attained through intimidation — directed not only at other residents but at Belinda as well. Also near the summit was Rose Goodman who, I decided, obtained her lofty status by claiming some high moral ground or at least more knowledge of the religious tenets to which we all, on the porch, had a connection.

I had once told Sarah that I was awed by people who were Orthodox or Hassidic.

> *"God must look upon them more favorably for so closely adhering to his wishes," I said. "Don't you think?"*
>
> *"Absolutely," she said, sarcastically. "God wants you to wear long, shaggy sideburns and dirty beards and he wants you to wear silly coats and hats, and most of all sell expensive diamonds mined with slave labor in South Africa like most of these people do. It surely gets them to heaven."*
>
> *It would not end there, I knew.*
>
> *"He also said that celibacy was a good idea, and not drinking milk with meat. That's great. And starving yourself to flush out all the sins, he just loves that. Do you know what he doesn't like though? Gefilte fish. He told me: tell them not to eat that junk for me."*

I closed my book, and pushed my chair toward the door. My hands hurt; they were chapped and dry from the wheel rubber, perhaps because I gripped it too tightly. "You will develop calluses," a physical therapist had told me. "People my age do not develop anything," I replied.

"Abe, where are you going?" Belinda called. "The dining room's not ready for lunch yet and the mail's not in until —" She looked at her watch. "Everyone will go with you when the mail comes in. Where are you going?"

"He's fine, leave him be," Hannah Cohen broke the stillness. I was grateful, and for an instant wanted to thank her. Instead, I arched my way beyond the empty nurses' station and inched my chair down the hall.

I rolled slowly along without a set destination, examining my surroundings, and becoming more and more troubled. Emunah's halls, I realized, were indistinguishable from those of the Beth Solomon Clinic where Sarah had been treated, or perhaps better put, made more comfortable as her time approached. Both institution's walls were pink and white, yet bland and without luster, and the linoleum floors were an identical gray and designed for easy travel in wheelchairs and gurneys. The medical monitors stored in each of the facilities' corridors, covered in dials and with cords streaming underneath, also confirmed the similarity. The only difference I could think of, in fact, was that at Emunah the equipment and the atmosphere were actually designed to do nothing more than ease the way to extinction. At Beth Solomon, for a short while anyway, the tools had been fleeting signs of hope.

I came to a portal, which I knew led to the convalescent wing, and rested there just outside the double-door entrance. I had no reason for being there, and I had certainly not planned to come. Still, I loitered momentarily, unsure of where to go next.

"Oye, Gott halp me pliss, pliss," a voice called from somewhere in the halls beyond the doorway. "Halp me, pliss, pliss." I couldn't tell whether the plea was a whisper spilling out from a room just on the other side of the entrance or a shout from a spot deeper in the bowels of the hospital. It didn't matter, however, where the words came from. The message — the prayer — was clear enough even if the voice was indistinct. Whoever it was, he was begging for death to come. The voice would not be heard on this earth much longer.

I proceeded back the way I had come, struggling still to reorder my thoughts. I considered maneuvering my way toward my room, but I glimpsed an aide at the end of a corridor and I headed the opposite way.

I found myself at Emunah's synagogue and, as I pushed my knees on the door, the stained-glass entry fell open. The darkness inside shrouded me, but as my vision improved, I could make out benches in rows and a small sculptured arc in the center of the rise glowing in the pale glimmer of the eternal light.

At a Sabbath service Sarah and I attended, a congregant stood and surprisingly questioned our rabbi in the midst of the Kaddish about the existence of God. The man was in mourning. "The existence of God is assumed in the scripture," the rabbi replied.

"Twenty years at the yeshiva and ten more of rabbinical school and that's what he comes up with? It's assumed?" Sarah said later, as we sat with some friends. "Apparently you don't have to be a genius to get access to the pulpit."

"Wouldn't it be better," her friend Meghan said, "if you just converted to Catholicism like the rest of us shiksas. You wouldn't have to listen to such nonsense. And," her face brightened, "then you and Abe would get the benefit of the hereafter and you could fawn over one another throughout eternity."

"Thanks," Sarah said, "but a lifetime is long enough."

I laughed. "Thanks a lot"

Why are you laughing?" she said. "You don't know why God exists either."

This called for some sarcasm of my own. "Because I was so lucky to have stumbled upon you, my demure sweet darling?"

She looked at me as if to say, "you're a jerk." "Children," she said. "That's how we know."

I smiled in the gray light of the chapel as the certainty etched into Sarah's expression that day returned to me. She was wrong, however, I thought suddenly. And the rabbi was indeed a fool. "Look at me," I said aloud, as if the rabbi was standing over me rubbing the tallises on his shawl. "Does God appear here today? Can I assume he is here, near me? No."

I was determined, then, to conjure up memories of my marriage. My plan was to begin with the train on which we met and wind a slow and deliberate path through the years, reviewing each moment of happiness as I went. I closed my eyes and prepared for waves of splendid reflections. Perhaps I'll fall asleep as I call the days back, I thought, and perhaps then I'll dream of those moments and they'll appear to me as if they're happening all over again. I settled in my chair.

Nothing came to mind.

I opened my eyes, stunned that the thoughts would not come.

"For God sakes," I mumbled, just to hear some sound. "How about the wedding."

At the reception, Sarah's father had risen, tapped his glass to ask for quiet, and when the room was silent, looked at me with a surprising seriousness. He's giving away his little girl, I thought. His pride and joy! His only daughter!

"Abe, I have only one piece of advice for you," he said, turning to me. "No matter what you do — under any circumstance — you can't give her back." He broke into a broad smile.

I propelled myself back through the corridors, and I implored to God as I went that my passage would go uninterrupted. I'm on the verge of becoming psychotic, I thought. My conversations, after all, were primarily in my head rather than with those around me, certainly a sign that I was less than fully competent, and I actually wanted nothing more than to settle in with my memories and be lost to this world forever, a sure sign of dementia.

To my surprise, I headed toward the porch. From a distance I could see that the card table was unoccupied, and that the couch near the television was vacant so I coasted inside. The windows to the gardens below, I convinced myself, and the comfort of my book, would evoke sweet memories. I needed only some breathing room, a little air, perhaps some light. The porch was not so horrible if it could be occupied alone.

"A human being," a voice said, close by, startling me. A hand with swollen knuckles was thrust into my face. "Samuel Levine Hersh, here. How are you?" I did not reach for the hand, but he grasped my forearm gently, lifted my palm into his and shook a greeting. I was stunned that he was there, and shocked that I had not noticed him.

"You've got pains," he said, knowingly. "Oye, don't I know it. These ankles," he pointed at his feet, "locked right up. I can't walk without this cane, and even then I walk like an ostrich. Eh, don't worry, that should be the worst thing that ever happens."

"Abraham Gilman," I mumbled. I pulled my hand away.

"This is such a pleasure to meet you. Do I call you Abraham? Abe?"

"Abe."

"Everyone calls me Sam. Eh, I actually prefer Samuel, but who's asking? When I was a kid they called me Leevie, but no one has called me that for years. Well, I'm talking on and on. We'll leave it at Sam."

He wore a suit, albeit one that was poorly tailored. Such attire was just not worn to the porch or anywhere else at Emunah. I had not, in fact, seen a suit since I left the hospital, and though I recalled a nurse speaking to me about sprucing up my apparel, the informal dress around the porch had not registered until now. Had he been clothed in pajamas or a medical smock, it occurred to me, his appearance would have been less surprising.

The suit itself was brown and the jacket had wide lapels and hung snugly from his rounded shoulders down to sleeves that seemed too tight. His trousers, too, looked more appropriate for someone several sizes smaller than he.

He pulled a chair over. "Some nurse, she tells me to come out here. I just arrived this morning, but she tells me the place to make friends is here on the porch. I've been standing here for half an hour. You're the first person I've seen. Not even a cockroach came in to say hello."

How could I avoid becoming his confidante?

"They play cards here, that much I see." He nodded his head in the direction of the table. "And television. They watch television." He contemplated his surroundings. "Esther, she said to me, she said this Emunah, do you think you'll like it? There are things for you to do there? I told her what else can I do? What choice do I have? It takes me an hour to get to the bathroom. Help is what I need but who has the money to get it in the house? Esther my dear sister, the widow. The poor thing. She gets along better than I do, though. Her husband, Arnold Scheff — did you know him? — No? Left her very well off. Anyway, she knows I'm not a good sitter. I like to do."

I nodded as if I were interested.

"I have a niece too. Brilliant. She's a doctor, my brother Ron's daughter. Ron passed away several years ago. Anyway, she said she would come visit and keep an eye on my ankles. I don't know about you, but when they stiffen up, the pain, oye the pain is terrible. Maybe I can get her to look at those legs. What happened to you?"

"I fell."

He looked surprised by my tone. "Oh, such a disaster this growing old. Anyone else hurt?" He seemed genuinely concerned. "I understand," he whispered. "This, I won't mention again." He squeezed my arm gently. "I apologize. I shouldn't pry. Your problems are not my problems."

Harry shuffled inside the doorway, followed by the other card players, all talking at once. Finally, Harry noticed that Hersh and I were monitoring the argument.

"And who the hell are you?" He spoke as if gravel rose from his throat.

"Hersh," one of the card players offered, "It's Hersh, Harry." He held another man by the elbow for balance. "Belinda told us about him."

Harry began to move toward us. I felt Hersh look over to me. There was no need for me to help him, though, I reasoned. First of all, I did not know what Harry wanted; more important, I was discouraged that Harry was about to invade my privacy as well.

"You Hersh?" Harry asked.

"Leevie Hersh, yes."

"I thought his name was Sam," Harry growled. "You don't know what the hell you're talking about half the time."

"I'm a kidder. It is Sam, actually," Hersh admitted.

"What, are you so senile you don't know your own name?" Harry shook his head in disgust. "Just like the rest."

"Samuel Levine Hersh. Leevie is a nickname from a long time ago."

Harry came closer, between Hersh's chair and mine. He wanted to bend down but he grabbed his back in pain. "This little Jewish kid comes home from school one day," he said, as if confiding in us. "He's all excited, and he says, 'Mama, I got the part of the husband in the school play.' " Harry paused. "The mother looks up at him and says 'oye dear dat's vunderful, keep working; next year you'll get a speaking part.' "

Hersh laughed delightedly. Harry stood up straight with a broad grin. "My son told me that one last Thursday," he said. "I didn't want to speak too loud. Some of these women around here think my boy's too loud." He coughed and winced.

Hersh put his arm on Harry's back. "Very good. Very good. Professional delivery too, like a real comedian. I didn't mean to be confusing, by the way. My name's Sam. That's what everyone calls me . . . now." He shook Harry's hand. "Abe and I were telling old stories and I remembered that old nickname. Sometimes I'm better off if I just keep quiet. So, anyway, it's a pleasure to meet you."

"Come with me, Mr. Hersh," Belinda said, helping him out of his seat. "I want you to meet the others." She placed her arm through his and led him toward Maury. Harry followed, to my relief.

Why had Belinda had taken such a keen interest in this new arrival, I wondered. Who was he to be guided about like a dignitary?

They reached the television. Watching their expressions, I thought the others seemed confused by him. Why did his obviously natural friendliness make everyone wary? Is it envy? Was it that he was still capable of displaying animation; that he still had energy? They are mad they are being disturbed, that's all. I'm thinking too much.

The television screen turned suddenly gray and then blank. A flurry of protests ensued.

"Oye, the nerve," a woman shrieked at Hersh.

"Are you soft in the head?" several others shouted.

There was also no doubt that Hersh had deliberately shut off the set. He dropped his shoulders, exhaled, and then glanced around at the angry faces before him. "I thought we might meet, that's all. I shouldn't have assumed. I apologize." He waited to be forgiven. When no one spoke up, he reached down and turned the set back on. "I'm Sam Hersh," he said softly. He saw Hannah Cohen and studied her for a moment. She smiled as he went past her. I think he winked as if there were an instant connection between them.

Sarah would have liked this man.

"I'm trying to engage you in conversation," I remember she said to me one day while I was grading papers.

"Uh huh."

"I want you to talk to me! I have nothing to do right now and I want to talk. You know, a discussion? You have heard of this? A little repartee? Light banter back and forth? A chat? Shoot the breeze? A heart to heart? ? Tête-à-tête?"

"Mmm," I shrugged. "I can't do it. . . . I'm boring."

"Wow," she said, smiling. "There's nothing I can say to that."

"Eh, do you play cards, Sam?" Harry said, dissolving the memory.

"No, I never have."

"The way things work around here," Maury interrupted, "you can't play cards, you're no good; you ask to be helped — for some tea, you're no good; you want to talk, they tell you to close your mouth. It's always, Maury, who cares about Maury? Nobody . . . Here . . . I can walk around for an hour before anyone gives me a seat. You want to sit? You can sit here." He pointed with a trembling hand to an unoccupied chair nearby. "Go ahead. It's all right. Maury Margolis, for one, won't complain. Go ahead."

Oye, I thought.

"Thank you, but no," Hersh said. "I'm tired now. I'm going to my room to rest." He made his way to the door, then turned, his head at a crooked angle as if he were deep in thought. Squinting, he peered at Hannah Cohen, his stare indicating he knew something the rest of us did not.

Hannah clearly sensed his scrutiny.

"I'm Sam Hersh," he said, his expression dissolving into a smile. "We didn't meet formally."

"My name is Hannah," she replied. "Hannah Cohen."

"It's very nice to meet you." He turned to face her.

"And you as well."

"So, what are you reading?"

"*The Chosen* by Chaim Potok," she said, lifting the book so he could see the cover. "Have you read it?"

"Have you gotten to the part where the kid gets hit in the face with the ball?"

She nodded. "It was a nice way to have the traditional and the contemporary collide."

"Now that, I never thought of. To me, it was just an unusal way for two people to meet," he said. "That, I will have to think about."

Without further incident he was gone down the hall.

The air had a dank quality on the porch the next morning. A breeze outside rustled the pines against the gray sky, and seemed almost to sift through the walls. I thought of how

Sarah might have closed her eyes on such a day, listening to the rain rattle against the panes. Her image crystallized.

> *"I swear it. I saw him!" Sarah said. "One second he's reviewing the sounds of each letter, and then he just looked up; his eyes opened really wide; he looked down and he got it. He started to read. You think I'm lying but it happened just like that."*
>
> *"There's a teacher's moment for you," I said, offering encouragement.*
>
> *She squinted at me. "That wasn't one of my students, that was Eisenhower."*

Belinda was shouting to Hannah from the nurses' station. "Dr. Luu told me that the Chinese word for boy has one of those scribbly symbols and also the Chinese word for girl, but if you put the two symbols together it makes —"

I couldn't hear her finish because Harry had won the pot in the card game and began to shout with glee, drowning out all other conversations.

"So, you like this Dr. Luu?" Hannah asked Belinda.

"He is happily married to Mrs. Luu," Belinda replied. "I just thought what he told me about those words was interesting and cute."

"A girl needs to be married," Gertie Neustadt wheezed. "This job can't pay you any money, cleaning up our tables and listening to us kvetch all day long. Go out. Find someone for yourself. Looks come; looks go. You are not so terrible to look at. What could be so bad?"

Belinda walked toward a patient asleep in her wheelchair.

"Any more numbing in the feet?" a man asked Rose Goodman from the other side of the room, near the terrarium. I looked over to see a lanky gentleman in a dress shirt and bow tie walking, on spindly legs, away from Rose, not waiting for a response. I remembered I had seen him in the same spot during my initial visit, though I had not given his presence much thought. He had perfectly groomed gray hair, and his clothes seemed meticulously cleaned and pressed. I could have mistaken him for a member of the staff or the administration if not for his teetering walk.

"No, Dr. Nathan, but thank you for asking," Rose said. He had already left the room.

"Abe . . . You're reading. I wanted to bother you. Just for a second, just for a moment. But I'll come back. Later, when it's more convenient, I'll come back." Hersh was leaning down behind me holding the handles to my chair. "It's more about my sister, Esther. Something you can hear later. Not to bother now." He shrugged.

I wish she were here to listen to you, I thought. "What is it?"

"Well, I've spoken to a few people, Belinda too, as a matter of fact, and well, my sister Esther, I think I told you about her yesterday. She's the one who said I'm not a sitter. Do you remember?"

I nodded.

"Yes, so she suggested — she thought it might be a wise idea to get involved with something. She thought an activity, a part-time job, a charity. Something. After her husband died she didn't have to work, and she took up some causes to keep busy." He looked at me for a response, but I had none to give. I tried to hide my exasperation.

"The people here," he went on with renewed enthusiasm. "I thought we might do something as a group instead of just sitting. Too much sitting goes on here."

He had on the same suit he had worn the day before; his appearance was that of a man depleted by age and the boredom that developed once he became infirm.

"I thought we could put our *keppeles* together. A few of us, and see if we could come up with something. Something maybe for charity, something else maybe. Esther, she says it's good for the soul. Or maybe we could help some people with their businesses. I owned a hardware store for forty-five years. Forty-five years in the same store, and thank you to God, I never went hungry."

"I can't help you. I was just a teacher," I said.

"A teacher? Wonderful! Marvelous! You must be a smart one. Anyway, Maury thought it might be a good idea too. To do something. Mrs. Cohen thought she might help too."

My calm had run out. "Help with what?" I demanded. "How would she know if she wanted to help when you haven't suggested anything?" I understood that his purpose in listing Hannah Cohen, among those who might volunteer in some philanthropic enterprise, was to bolster its status. After all, she was one of the few capable and informed residents and everyone acknowledged this fact. I was, nevertheless, exasperated that he could not explain his proposal more effectively, and even more irked that instead of describing what he had in mind, he was telling me first who was allied with him, as if that would sway me.

He thought for a moment. "Well, we can certainly use the telephone. We could make calls — for Israel — they are still planting trees. The United Jewish Appeal, Hope, CARE or maybe — I think it is called the Association of the Retired." He thought for a moment. "I saw a commercial on the television for it once. It's a group of retired people who help out."

"I'm not interested," I declared. "I was a schoolteacher. I know nothing about business, and I don't like talking on the telephone. I don't like talking at all, in fact. I'm old. Exhausted. Look at me. I'm alone. No home.

Crippled. Now you want me to sit on the telephone all day and call strangers?"

"So, it was a thought." He moved away. I felt as though he'd offered me condolences with his feigned despondence. When he reached Maury Margolis, he began to chatter again as if our conversation had not even occurred.

"I just want to be alone," I called after him. "Is that too much to ask?"

FEBRUARY 1948

"I hear my boys showed you how to play the game after all," Officer Creen grinned as he put a package of Standard Electric bulbs on the counter. "It pays, you see, to have the Good Lord on your side."

"I think the Lord was on our side," Elie responded, "you just had Whitey Cleary." The officer laughed and reached into his pockets, which Elie knew were empty. "I'll put these on the station account," Elie assured him.

"Don't bother yourself. Truth is we don't really need them anyway. I just wanted to have a little fun, that's all." He patted his bulging stomach. "It feels good to be a winner." He lowered his voice. "They tell me, by the way, that Mochiber is one big . . . well; he can actually shoot the ball. You're right, of course; he's not Roger Cleary's boy, but then, as old Roger says, who is?"

Elie replaced the bulbs on the shelf and walked back to the counter where Isaac Gurlock stood, bent over Elie's book. "It seems quiet today, no?" Isaac asked, without looking up. He turned the book over to look at the cover. "*Composition and Journalism,* this is a book to read?" He eyed Elie suspiciously. "Or are you planning another little writing caper? Like with the goyim."

A young Hassidic couple with a baby came into the

store, followed by a large grim woman, Mrs. Geffen. They disappeared down different aisles; Elie could hear the couple at the back of the store discussing their purchases.

"Isaac," Mrs. Geffen said, as she circled the rack of shovels near the door. "Good morning. You have paint? I need paint. Are you the Wasserman boy?" she asked Elie.

"Irma, you ask him if he is the Wasserman boy every time you come in," Isaac scolded her. "You've been talking to Mrs. Zaretsky again." Mrs. Geffen shrugged. "The Zaretskys, they are old. They live in an old house that needs work. Elie doesn't have time to help everyone that comes in. He works. He goes to school. He has his own mother to look after. Paint, I can sell you. Would it be so terrible to ask your own boy to help?"

"Morris is too busy. He's studying, as you know. You think he has time to paint walls when he's studying? Besides, this boy has time to play games and be reckless at the expense of Rabbi Kishenev's daughter, so —"

"The boy can't play basketball at night?" Isaac turned to Elie. "Reckless at the expense of Dina Kishenev. That doesn't sound good."

"Yes, he practically killed her, from what I understand from Mrs. Shetzel. The rabbi is worried that there will be permanent scarring. And even more worried Bernard will look elsewhere if her nice face does not return. Such a *shayna punum* the child had until yesterday. Why a nice boy would do such a thing, I can't understand."

The Hassidic couple approached the counter. The husband held a ball peen hammer and a box of brads. "It was an accident. That's all. The girl's fine."

"Why then was he at the rabbi's afterwards begging the rabbi and Mrs. Kishenev to accept his apology?"

"You see that's the difference," the Hassidic man argued. "Rebbe Liebenshul wouldn't make anyone beg for such a thing. And Bernard will accept anyone unconditionally. She could have a face like a lizard and it would make no difference to the rebbe's son. It was an accident, Isaac, rest assured." He paid for the tool and fasteners.

"Honestly," Elie heard the Hassidic man say to Isaac, "Rebbe Liebenshul and Rabbi Kishenev are so different. Sometimes I wonder if it can be they are of one faith."

"Hush, now. You don't know Rebbe Kishenev," the man's wife said. "Anyway, the rebbe says they're good friends. Perhaps it's only the congregants who think they're so different."

"I think you should listen," Isaac responded. "Everything said isn't always true. For instance, I'm sure you're right. It was an accident with the girl. He's a good boy. He wouldn't do such a thing on purpose."

Elie thought about what Dina had told him on their walk home: The congregations were wary of one another. Their differences, no matter how subtle, separated them.

At the front of the store, Elie heard the door swing open again. "Isaac, Isaac," the visitor pleaded. It was Sy Kaplan, the florist. "Is the boy here?" Kaplan began to scour the store. As he searched he stammered. "Oye, with a ball Isaac, he clopped her. Mangled he left her. Barely alive, Lester Miffmacher told me." He turned the corner and located Elie. "There!"

He approached Elie menacingly. "You chose the rebbe's daughter to take out your frustrations? What kind of boy would do this? You and I, Elie, I thought we knew each other. How do I explain this?"

"Ha," Mrs. Geffen responded. "He'll tell you it was an accident. If you ask me, Hy, the Butcher of Hecht, he put him up to it. Nobody told me, but that's my guess."

"It was an accident, Sy, honest. I was shooting at the basket and she was walking by. She looked up."

"Elie, we're going to be late. You're going to be late." It was Yudie shouting from the front of the store.

Elie looked at the clock.

"Did you apologize?" Sy asked.

"I walked her home to be sure she was all right and I begged Rebbe Kishenev's forgiveness. Mrs. Kishenev, also."

"This is a serious matter," Sy warned. "Accident or no, tonight you should go back and make sure she's all right. Such a nice gesture will get around too and then everyone will know you didn't mean it. Mrs. Shetzel will make sure." He held a hand to his cheek. "Come to the store. I'll give you a flower to take to her. Isaac, he will pay for it, I am sure."

Elie was glad for the excuse to leave. He grabbed his book, shouted a farewell to Isaac Gurlock, and promised to come back later that afternoon. Yudie waited on the sidewalk with Joel Mochiber. "Gurlock managed to get up in time for you to go to school. And I thought living forty years in the desert was a miracle," Yudie remarked. "Helf's must have run out of wine."

"Don't be disrespectful," Joel scolded.

"I like being disrespectful. Besides, telling the truth isn't being disrespectful. It's being honest. I'm honest through and through. You have to admit that. Right?" Elie was not listening. "All right, forget that." Yudie paused. "So, tell us already. We want to hear all the ugly details of your excommunication."

"Did the rebbe scream?" Joel asked. "Oye, I can't imagine what Dina's mother must have said. Well, at least you're still alive. Mazel Tov. That alone is a miracle."

"It wasn't so terrible. They were very nice," Elie stated. "I'm going to go back tonight. I want to make sure she's all right."

"As if you wouldn't hear about it if she wasn't," Yudie argued. "As if I am not going to hear about it just for being near you when it happened. He stopped suddenly.

"What! You're going back? You must be soft. Why would you do such a thing? You said you were sorry. That's enough."

For several blocks, they walked in silence. Elie thought about Dina trying so hard to stay mad at him before giving up.

"What did you talk about on the way home?" Joel asked. "Could she walk? Yudie said she wouldn't walk all the way."

"She talked about Bernard, mostly," Elie admitted, "and she talked about the synagogues a little." His friends looked at him. "About how Rabbi Kishenev wants to bring everyone together."

"And about how she and Bernard will break down the barriers between the two congregations," Yudie said, sarcastically. "I have heard this every day since I first started reading the Haftorah. Together with the Talmud and the Mishnah, we heard about this marriage. The "Union," I had a teacher call it once. She really took you into her confidence. I'm surprised this proposed marriage hasn't been required reading in even your heathen school."

"I'd heard something about it. A little."

"You spend too much time at Gurlock's, honestly," Yudie said.

"Did you actually see the rabbi?" Joel asked. "You dropped her off, that's all, right? Did you go inside?"

Elie was surprised by Joel's worried tone. "Mrs. Kishenev asked me in for tea. The whole family was there. I think it was the whole family."

"And what did you talk about when you were having tea?" Joel wondered.

"Are we talking about Rabbi Kishenev here or Harry Truman?" Yudie said. "The way you talk, you'd think he had dinner at the White House with Gandhi and Ben Gurion. He had tea."

"You were the one who wanted to rush over here. But go ahead, blame me now for asking questions."

While they argued, Elie thought back to Dina's imaginary description of Bernard carrying her home and keeping a watch by her bed as she recovered. He did not know Bernard, but he pictured him as tall and thin and distant. "I'd like to meet this Bernard Liebenshul," Elie said.

"Why?" Joel asked.

"I don't think she really likes him that much."

As the darkness came to Mattapan, Elie stood outside Adas Yeraim. There was a voice coming from the synagogue, and Elie wondered if it was Rabbi Kishenev giving blessings to a minyan of listeners. He closed his eyes.

The night was clear but cool; Elie pulled his coat closer. He wanted to see Dina, he knew that, but he was concerned that Bernard might be there and that he would be intruding or that Dina would refuse his apology or be mad that he had not left her alone to heal. He decided Mrs. Kishenev would likely not be angry with him, and he considered leaving the rose he had purchased from Sy Kaplan — and his good wishes — with her.

Elie walked to the rear door and rang the bell. As he heard footsteps approaching, he decided that he should have knocked instead.

"Elie!" Mrs. Kishenev said. She gestured for him to enter. "With the way my daughter goes on sometimes, well, for some reason, I thought we might not get to see you again. Please come in."

From another room Elie heard one of the children ask who was at the door. "I probably shouldn't have rung the bell," Elie apologized. "I hope I didn't interrupt Rabbi Kishenev."

"If all these children in the next room don't disturb him, a little ringing, I promise you, he won't even hear.

Here, let me take your coat. He should be done soon anyway." She lowered her voice. "They'll get hungry, soon. Then the praying will end."

"I shouldn't stay too long," Elie said. "I just wanted to make sure Dina was all right." He glanced at the flower in his hand and wondered if he should be embarrassed. He wasn't. "Is she?"

"You shouldn't worry yourself. Already, six people today have told me it was her own fault. That she was walking and reading, as always, and not watching where she was going." Mrs. Kishenev took Elie's hand in both of hers. "This is a habit we both have to work on," she whispered. She let go of Elie's fingers and patted his wrist. "Otherwise someday it won't be a basketball," she said loudly, "it will be a truck."

"Maybe Bernard will keep an eye on her." Elie was trying to be polite.

"That, anyway," she said, pointing to the rose, "will make her feel better. For two years she's been carrying on about Bernard Liebenshul. Not one flower in all that time."

"He's probably busy, that's all. I'm sure he never popped her with a ball, either."

"He is too busy to make my Dina happy," she sighed. "That much I know. She knows too. It's her father who seems not to see it. Eh, this is another story."

Elie looked toward the door as Judah turned the corner. "You're still not Bernard."

"Judah, this is Elie Wasserman. You met him last night. I'm sure you remember."

"Yes, Mama," he said, "but Dina said it was Bernard at the door. And she said she was glad he finally came to take away some of her pain and angels. Why would he take away her angels?"

"Anguish," Mrs. Kishenev pronounced.

"Are you here to take her an . . . ann-gish?" Judah asked Elie. "I don't think she wants it, so you can probably have it. She was going to give it to Bernard anyway."

Elie put his hand on Judah's head and felt the soft silk of his yarmulke. "I was going to give her a flower instead," he confided. "Maybe you could give this to your sister, and see if it makes her feel better." Judah's eyes grew wide and he grabbed the rose.

"Oye, my children have no manners. You better follow him or he'll take all the credit for your flower." She turned toward the kitchen. "It's beautiful. Sy has nice flowers. You can tell a Sy Kaplan flower just by looking." Pointing with two fingers, she let Elie know in which direction to go to find Dina.

Elie passed through a dim hallway, following the children's voices. There were books everywhere. One, *Journalism and Literature,* by Boynton Henry Walcott caught his eye. He wondered if the Kishenevs ever let anyone borrow their books.

He found Dina in the study, sitting in a large stuffed chair with a child squeezed between the armrests on either side. Judah still held the rose in his fist. Dina had a children's book open in her lap.

"Do you know what my friend Kai told me?" Reyna said to Elie, closing the book so Dina would stop reading. "She's at the playground. We play sometimes. She's Chinese."

"What did she say?" Elie asked.

"She told me that in Chinese, there's a squiggly thing for girl and that there's another squiggly thing for boy. But she told me that if you put the squiggles together, it makes the word 'perfect.' "

"What a great sentiment," Dina said, peering at Elie before turning away, embarrassed. "That's interesting, I mean."

Elie studied Dina. Even in the dim light he could see that she had two black eyes. The swelling was gone, and he was glad for that. The bruises, however, were clear.

"I know. I look like a witch," she declared. "I have the face of a monster." She hid her face in her hands. "I might as well have boils and scars covering my skin. Or be burned at the stake like Joan of Arc and have my flesh charred. I'd be less hideous and deformed than I am now." She fell back into the chair. "I was not all that pretty to begin with and now I look like Grendel, the monster Grendel."

"Dina," Judah whispered, "I told you he brought this flower. Mama liked it! And you are pretty. Bernard won't mind your face. No more saying that."

"I just came to make sure you were okay. And to tell you again I'm sorry."

She continued to hold her hands over her face. "My friend Naomi Moscow couldn't even look at me today. 'Your future,' she said, 'destroyed by God's own hand. A tragedy of proportions beyond any in any written work or the mind of man,' were her exact words. She suggested self-exile."

"Mama said you'd heal," Reyna argued.

Mrs. Kishenev called to Judah and Reyna from the kitchen.

"Dina's very sad," Reyna instructed Elie, with a serious face. "She's sad Bernard hasn't come to see her or pulled down the telephone to talk to her." They left for the kitchen, Judah still holding the flower in his grip.

"I'm sure he's been busy, that's all," Elie said when the children had gone. "Talmud study is very difficult."

"I know, I just thought this might have given him a reason to come." She sighed. "It isn't really my face, though, I know that. He just loves his studies. Rabbi Liebenshul demands it."

"Yudie asked me how you were."

Dina looked up. "He's usually so mean to me."

They each waited for the other to speak. "What did you tell him?" Dina finally asked. "Did you tell him I was mangled and repulsive? And that I was destined to live alone and destitute."

"You sure are full of tragedy," Elie said. "No, I didn't say that." He grew serious. "I told him you were still beautiful."

"You did? You really said that?"

"You shouldn't listen to your friend Naomi, you know. I think both of you read too many *Harper's* magazines."

Dina was quiet for a moment. "I know it was an accident at the gym last night. And I'm sorry I carried on so. Everyone says I get too dramatic. Bernard says it's a habit I have to break. He said that a rabbi's wife must be calm and polite at all times. I wasn't very calm or polite to you last night. I'm sorry for that. Bernard wouldn't have been happy with me." She pursed her lips. "You were probably not too enchanted either."

Elie wanted to tell her he was. "It was a dumb thing to do," he said instead. "I was too far away and there were too many people around. I should have tried a pass back to Joel."

"Bernard doesn't play basketball," Dina said. "I don't know what he does for fun."

"I would like to meet Bernard someday. Yudie says he's already very well respected and very smart."

"Yudie Kosasky said that too?" She squinted at Elie to determine whether he was telling the truth. He could see that her face ached. "Yudie said no such thing. You made that up."

"He doesn't usually say nice things. He wasn't very nice to you last night. I thought he could have been nicer, considering you got hit. Anyway, he did say that about Bernard."

A crestfallen expression fell over her face and she rested her head back against the cushions and closed her eyes. Elie watched her in what light there was. Even the bruised skin did not affect her gentle features. She seemed almost fragile.

"Thank you for my flower. It's beautiful. Do you think dear Judah will ever give it back to me?"

"The flower was for Judah," Elie said, feigning confusion.

Dina winced when she tried to pretend she was angry.

"His eyes got so big when he saw it, I had to hand it to him. He would have been madder than you are at me if I didn't let him bring it in. I'm just glad Sy got all the thorns. He doesn't usually anymore. I was sure I was about to injure another member of your family."

"I'm not mad at you. I won't prattle anymore. I promise." Her voice grew softer. "You've been very nice to me."

"Sy told me that if someone's mad at you, you bring them one rose. If they're sick, you bring them a dozen. Now that I know you're not mad, I better go back and get the other eleven."

"I'm not sick, either. Just deformed."

"A dozen," Elie said, mimicking Sy Kaplan, "better than any medicine; all ills are cured, no matter how serious." Dina seemed to sink lower into the chair. "Okay, so he's a better salesman than he is a doctor."

"No. I think Sy's wonderful. He's very nice to Mama. And the flower is beautiful," she said. "I'm just forlorn, that's all. Forever to be saddled with loneliness and the knowledge that I've broken my father's heart. Even beautiful flowers can't cure that."

"How did you break your father's heart?" he asked. "I

thought it was a broken nose. And I'm pretty sure it was my fault."

Dina sighed. "My father will be heartbroken if Bernard changes his mind. My father, he's counting on me. Sometimes, though, I think Bernard would be just as happy to marry Elsie Rovner. She's much quieter than I am. And she was always much prettier, too, even before I looked like Bela Lugosi." She sunk further. "My father said we shouldn't get married unless we loved one another. When I told him we had learned to love each other, he told everyone it was ordained; that he knew God would intervene and eventually find favor with the marriage."

Elie knew she was not telling him the truth. He was certain she was not in love with Bernard.

"Our being in love was everything my father had hoped for and," she took a deep breath "and he had his daughter's . . . well, I was happy too. He was so filled with joy. He was. And now I may have ruined everything. My poor father will be heartsick."

"I'm the one that hit you with the ball. You didn't ruin anything. Besides Bernard will come by soon. And if he doesn't, then you shouldn't marry him anyway. He may be well respected, but he'd be kind of a jerk."

Dina giggled, then caught herself. "I wish it were that simple. Anyway, as I said yesterday, I believe it's permanent scarring he worries about. It just wouldn't be proper for the rebbe's wife to be disfigured. It would be very embarrassing for Bernard to have his children raised by an ogress. Even my father would probably agree. It just wouldn't be proper."

A door creaked open somewhere in the house and the sound of the conversations from behind the walls of the synagogue distracted them. The rabbi's voice issuing farewells was clear. Elie also heard Mrs. Kishenev call to one of the congregants, wishing his wife a speedy recovery. When everyone had gone, the rabbi requested a pot of tea. His voice sounded tired.

"They take good care of each other, my mother and father," Dina said softly. "Does your mother miss your father?"

"Yes. We have one picture and she still keeps his uniform from the first war, but it hurts her to talk about him. We don't know much about what happened to him. My mother thinks he's going to come home; show up at our door one day. She doesn't believe he's gone."

"That's sad. More than anything else I know that my parents need one another. My parents were chosen for each other by my grandparents. They knew from a very young age they'd be married. Mama says they were always friends after that. Bernard and I aren't very friendly."

"Bernard may not be," Elie defended her.

Dina nodded. "When I was little, I thought all marriages were arranged. I prayed that Papa would find someone for me who would just be nice to me."

Elie sensed her gloom that this was all she could expect.

"I even asked Mama once whom they had picked for me and when she told me I was to make my own choice, I thought she was teasing me. A girl couldn't pick for herself, I thought. I told her I would never know whom to choose. Once, I even begged her to choose for me. She told me I'd wake up one night and just know who was perfect, because part of the choice was knowing the person I had chosen had selected me also."

Elie thought he saw her expression melt into contentedness as she imagined some great love. She peered up at him as if to tell him she understood it was possible, then steeled herself.

"I remember her exact words: 'You will make everyone very happy with your choice,' she said." Dina put up her hands and seemed to want to block off her imagination. "I'm sorry. I know I talk too much. I barely know you and I'm telling you these silly things."

Elie was dizzy with enchantment. "My mother tells me all the time that she knows my father is still alive. She believes the connection between them was so strong, she would know if he had died, even if no one had told her."

Dina pulled her sweater more tightly around her. "My friend Naomi Moscow once told me she thought it was impossible to choose the person that was exactly right for you. She said there's only one perfect person for everybody and you could never possibly find them. Your perfect person could live in Paris or Peru or maybe even Palestine. You can never even hope to be in the same country with them, let alone meet them."

Elie didn't respond, but he stared at her as if to say she was wrong. He was sure she understood. They were there together now.

"The only thing you can do, she told me, is to try to choose someone who'll be nice to you and take care of you." She blinked away tears. "Look at the mess I've made."

From the kitchen, Mrs. Kishenev called them to join Rabbi Kishenev for tea. As they moved down the hall their arms touched.

"Mr. Wasserman, you are kind to call on us a second time," the rabbi declared when they came into the kitchen. "Perhaps a more sensible friend than Naomi Moscow will relieve us of this talk of lives lived in solitude and permanent disfigurement." The rabbi sat at the table with Judah on his lap. Judah still held the flower in one hand. In the other he held several cubes of sugar that the rabbi, a moment later, confiscated and returned to the bowl.

"And a flower from Sy Kaplan. One rose for anger. A

dozen for sickness. Sy's a wise businessman. I think there's always more sickness than true anger. Though in this case, I am surprised he didn't sell you a dozen, just in case."

"Papa," Mrs. Kishenev scolded him, "your daughter is neither sick nor angry. Elie is just being kind."

"My daughter has a fiancé, Mr. Wasserman," the rabbi announced, "though this, I'm sure you already know. Of course, the boy is even less able to communicate than his father, if such a thing can be."

"Rabbi!" Mrs. Kishenev said sharply.

"Papa!" Dina said.

"The boy brings a flower. He has a right to know the girl is already promised. Is that so terrible? I am just saying —"

"Bernard didn't bring a flower," Judah said. "Elie did."

"And how did you end up with a flower intended for your sister?" the rabbi asked.

"I asked for Judah's help," Elie said.

"And I asked him to carry it for me and hold it," Dina added.

The rabbi looked up at them. "Ah," he said gently to Judah, "your defenders have arrived. You're a good boy to have such friends."

Elie was glad to be with this family, and pleased to be in concert with Dina in the rabbi's eyes, even for something so inconsequential.

"He's here to check on your daughter's condition," Mrs. Kishenev lectured. "You should be nice to him."

"So, you're right. My lips are closed."

"I thought I better come and make sure Dina was all right, Rebbe," Elie said. "We just met yesterday. That's all. I've never met Bernard, but all of my friends tell me he's going to be a great man someday. The flower was just to apologize." Elie looked at Dina and for an instant he thought he saw a look of abandonment. He felt, suddenly, as if he should not have defended Bernard, as if he had broken a secret pact between them. They had not spoken about it, but he sensed she wanted him to somehow intervene.

"Old religious men can say things they shouldn't," the rabbi said, watching his daughter's expression as well. "The pay isn't good, but we are usually forgiven our intrusions. Please accept my apology."

From down Blue Hill Avenue the bells of St. Anselm's Covenant rang seven times. In the kitchen everyone sipped their tea. Judah kissed his father's gray beard.

"I'm blessed with a wonderful family," the rabbi said, rubbing his son's head. "A bit eccentric at times, perhaps," he ventured with a quick glance at Dina, who, Elie could see, pretended to be annoyed, "but yes, wonderful. In the Talmud, there is a saying: He who honors his wife with righteousness leads his sons and daughters along the proper path.

Your mother, too, is a righteous woman," the rabbi continued. "This much I can tell about her from your manners. You, too, are blessed." He scratched his beard. "And I know that you are a charitable boy also. The neighborhood has been full of talk of your good character since last night. Again, anyway, I'm sorry. An old, tired man talks too much. You are kind to bring flowers. I know your intentions are noble." He leaned toward Elie as if to reveal a secret. "And I understand from Meyer Posner that you're clever with the goyim too!"

His wife's face tightened with anger.

"So, all right. Can I help it if the boy is clever? No."

"And what's so clever that you have to speak with such a tone," she scolded, "and use such terms that you've promised me not to teach your children. This is America, not the shtetel."

"Meyer Posner, he tells me that the parishes, all of the Catholic churches in Mattapan and Dorchester, every year they get together, and offer a prize — money no less — to one parishioner who writes the best essay. The Fathers, they pick the topic and everyone writes an essay. Of course the topic is always —" A look of warning passed from the rebbe's wife. "The topic always relates to the teachings of the Catholics, there. This year, Meyer Posner says, the topic has something to do with the Holy Ghost and who is this apparition? Of course, only those who have studied such things could write on such a topic, Posner says to me and I agree. Like the Talmud, it must take ten years of study to even write the first sentence on such a topic."

"And what?" Mrs. Kishenev asked.

"Under the name, Durham, Durham O'Brien?"

"Brian Durham," Elie said.

"Brian Durham. Using the name Brian Durham, he writes the essay, and he wins. The best essay he writes." He turned to Elie. "How could you know so much to write on a topic such as this?"

"I went to the library." Elie liked to tell this story. He was proud and thought his father would've been also.

"They didn't give you the prize, though," Dina said.

Elie shook his head.

"You win, but you do not win?" the rebbe asked. "And how does this work?"

"They checked the rules," Dina answered, quietly. "There was no rule that said he couldn't enter so, to keep him from winning, they decided that the award would go to him only if he could prove his name was Brian Durham. They gave the award to someone else."

Elie did not know how she knew so much about the incident, but was charmed and inspired that she did.

"And how much was this award that was stolen from you?" the rebbe asked.

"Five dollars," Elie said.

"Five dollars!" Mrs. Kishenev repeated. "Father Tierney should be ashamed of himself."

"It doesn't matter. It was just practice. I shouldn't have done it. I just wanted to see if I could write about something I knew very little about."

"Tell me," the rabbi inquired, "you were born in this country? Or are you transplanted, like the rest of us?"

"I grew up here," Elie replied. "My memory is that we have always, my mother and I, that is, lived in our apartment on Crossman Street, but I was born in Germany. In a city called Freiburg. It's a small city, in the south. I don't have any memory of it. We left when I was very young."

"Your father?" the Rabbi prodded.

"My father sent us here. He stayed behind." Elie paused. "I don't have a memory of my father either, really. I can feel him sometimes. Other times a face leaps into my head and I think it's him. But it always seems as if someone has just popped a dozen flashbulbs in my eyes. He's there, but I just can't see his face clearly."

Mrs. Kishenev pressed her lips together. "I'm sorry."

"Forgive me for asking, but what prompted this man to deliver his family and not to follow later? Why did he leave himself in such terrible danger?"

"My mother doesn't speak about my father. She hasn't told me much at all. She misses him so much. I think it's painful for her to talk about him. She's quiet. Sad, I think. She's still waiting for my father to knock on our door and come home."

No one spoke. He sipped his tea and sorted through what little he knew.

"I know a few things about him."

"Please tell me — us — about him," Dina said again, quietly.

"I know he was a journalist and that he worked for a

paper, the *Abenpost*. He reported on local politics, mostly. My mother still has a few articles. She keeps them in her jewelry box."

"Elie wants to become a journalist also," Dina interrupted, "and then perhaps a novelist or a poet." She bit her lower lip. Elie knew she had invented a history for him. "You'll probably spend years as an apprentice to a publisher of ill temper," she went on. "Learning your trade. Grinding out perfect prose, day after day, until he fires you for becoming a better writer than he ever was. Then you'll hide away until you finish the perfect work of literature. People will say: This is perfect literature. Every word brims with meaning. They will hail you and wave to you in the streets. You —"

"Dina!" Mrs. Kishenev scolded. "The boy could want a job, and a family and a quiet life. Maybe even go to shul once in a while."

Elie studied Dina's face and could see that she'd like that too. A tender calm came over him as he imagined them doing it together. "That's okay. I like that story."

There was quiet as the children slipped from the table and disappeared. Elie daydreamed about his father meeting Dina. He wanted to explain to her that even though he didn't know this man who helped bring him into the world, he was nevertheless guided by him, and somehow even nurtured by whatever little memory he had. "I think my father would have liked that for me."

"For my daughter, I apologize. Please go on," the rabbi requested.

"He fought in the First War and he was decorated." Elie waited for someone to ask a question, but no one did. "After he returned home, my mother told me, they said he . . . they called him," he paused, trying to remember the correct German. "*Hebraisch Held*. I think that's right. Anyway, that's what she said. The Hebrew Hero, I think it means. She never told me why he was decorated, but I guess there were some terrible battles that he fought; very bravely. I think he saved some other soldiers' lives."

"These are stories you should know," the rabbi advised. "You should require your mother to tell you."

"Hush, Papa," Mrs. Kishenev instructed. "The boy isn't finished."

"No, you're right," Elie went on. "But sometimes I can't make myself ask my mother to tell me more. Sometimes I think she feels that if she talks about him, he'll never come back. I don't want her to feel any worse than she already does."

"In our religion memories serve as the way to preserve someone in your heart even after they're gone. This much I know you know."

"Please finish," Dina said. She put her hand near Elie's. The urge to touch her made his breathing shallow. "Papa, let him finish."

Mrs. Kishenev nodded.

Emboldened, he went on. "I guess, after the war, my father was lucky enough to get a job at the *Abenpost,* and even though there were difficult times, my parents were able to take care of themselves and me." Elie realized he knew little about how his parents met and decided he would ask his mother more about their courtship. "The war had made things difficult all over Germany. I've read a lot about the years between the wars." Elie worried that Dina would think he was boasting, but she seemed spellbound.

"Just after I was born, there were riots in Berlin."

"Long before the Second War even started," the rabbi told Dina, "even then the Jews were blamed for the terrible problems in Europe. Always when things are bad, people blame us."

"Hitler had come to power by then," Elie explained,

combining what he had heard from his mother and what he had read. "The Reichstag had been burned. Hitler called for a boycott of all Jewish businesses. It would've been much worse — and this was only in 1933 — except that foreign governments complained. Eventually the boycott ended."

"And so your parents decided to leave?" Mrs. Kishenev asked.

"Not long after that. My mother says that my father watched carefully what was happening. Hitler began to enact laws to take jobs away from Jewish workers. Concentration camps were built and people were taken there and, my mother said girls in the street would scream things at her for no reason. *Utermensch,* they would say." He looked at Dina, who clearly did not understand the insult. "Monster. I guess a short time later there was a law that made being Aryan a requirement for writing for a newspaper in Germany. I think that's when my father decided we should go."

He noticed Dina was fascinated.

"My mother told me that one night during the boycott we were attacked by a group of men who threw stones and came at us with irons. On the way home from shul it was, on the Sabbath. My mother says they were about to kill us, these people we didn't even know. And they would have, she said, but one of the men recognized my father. Anyway, they stopped and even apologized, my mother said, because my father had been a soldier. *Der Hebraisch Held*. She doesn't say it, but I think that story is why my father sent us on ahead. I think he thought he could stop some of the killing himself, but he didn't want to risk something happening to my mother and me." Elie waited for questions. "My mother wishes, of course, that he'd just come with us."

"What year did you come?" asked the rabbi.

"We arrived in America in 1935. I was five. We lived in Chicago for a little while."

"And your mother had contact with your father after you arrived?"

Elie swallowed. His throat felt dry. "She says that she wrote letters every day. I have memories of her doing nothing but writing letters. There were probably thousands." He recalled an image from his childhood of his mother huddled over a dimly lit desk scribbling in German or in Yiddish. "She was desperate to let my father know where we were. We eventually made it to Chicago to stay with a cousin of my father's. In October of 1939 we came to Mattapan, but by then — she told me she finally began to post letters to everyone she knew in Freiburg. To tell them we had come to Mattapan. Friends, hospitals, even people she knew who didn't like Jews. She never received one word back after that. Nothing."

Mrs. Kishenev muttered something in Yiddish. "Not a word in all this time. The poor woman. How does she live?"

"Have you made inquiries about your father?" the rebbe asked.

"Inquiries?"

"To find out what happened to him?"

Elie nodded. "I went to the military, to the army, to see if they kept records or could obtain any records. The sergeant there told me to go to the National Archive Office instead or to the British Consulate's office. He said they might have more information. They were still looking for missing soldiers lost in the Pacific, he told me. He didn't have time to look for lost Jews." Elie remembered his exasperation. "One man in the consulate took my name and promised to call me if he learned of anything. He never did."

"Golems, all of them," Mrs. Kishenev sputtered.

"I went to the library to see if records of the camps had been published. There weren't any. Anyway, the truth is, I am afraid I might see his name somewhere. I don't know how I would tell my mother."

For several seconds no one spoke. "Mr. Wasserman," the rabbi finally announced, "your mother, I think, is much stronger than you know. More importantly, you should remember that your parents are your most precious gift. It is your parents that make you — that make all of us what we are. They give us life and foundation. Guide us and define us. Honor your mother and father. That is a commandment. You do your father no honor and your mother no benefit by having this mystery left unsolved. It may be too painful for your mother to search for the truth or to acknowledge it, but I promise you from my heart, she's waiting for this story to be concluded."

"To be concluded?" Elie asked.

"To be resolved," the rabbi clarified. "You should make it your work, your mission, to learn your father's fate. This is a matter of great importance. In the Torah are the words: 'Honor thy father and thy mother.' And later, the Proverbs tell us 'Honor the Lord with thy substance.' A subtle difference, but a difference, you see. My teachers explained the meaning of these words to be that it was of even more importance to honor and revere your parents than to honor God." He waited to allow his offering to be understood. "You honor God by showing charity, by using what you have to help those less fortunate than yourself. Honor the Lord with thy substance, you see, whatever it is, large or small. But the teachings are clear: Even if you have nothing, if you are destitute and accepting of charity yourself, you must still do whatever's necessary to honor your mother and father."

Everyone was silent. "There is a service," he went on, "it is run by the Red Cross. A woman named Frana Luftwantz heads the local office and she's supported by congregations in Mattapan, and in Dorchester, as well. The government helps, too, though only a little, not enough, if I may insert my feelings about this. Anyway, this service helps those looking for relatives and friends who were lost in Europe during the war. They have records. They have information that they've gathered from many sources to help people locate those whom cannot be found. Concentration camp records. Records of executions. Other records. They've gathered much. Well you should contact Frana Luftwantz."

"Where do I find her?" Elie's thoughts wavered between frustration and hopefulness. Did his mother know about this service? Why hadn't he heard of this before.

"Walk Hill Street, I believe. North of the Square. Go there. They'll help you. With luck you will meet my daughter's fiancé, as well. On occasion he helps there." The rabbi drained his tea. Outside, the bells tolled again. "Forgive me for going on and on. I'm tired. You've come to apologize and I've managed to deflect your good intentions with other concerns. For this you'll have to forgive me. Good night. I must check on the studies of my son. Come back again and visit us." He glanced up at his wife. "Perhaps Mr. Wasserman can be invited to the wedding. A suggestion, Harva; I'm just saying. The boy should know of her plans, that's all! So, slice out my tongue." He turned to Elie. "Visit with Frana Luftwantz. It's best that you do."

Elie stood. "I should go," he said, thinking about what the rabbi had told him. He had not heard of this service and he wondered why no one had told him about it.

"There's more tea," Dina said softly. "You don't have to go."

"Your father's right, I should. My mother will wonder what happened to me."

"Why don't you let Elie out the front," Mrs. Kishenev

suggested. "It's late and the lights are better on Fessenden Street. Dina, get Elie his coat."

Dina led Elie through the synagogue, down the dim aisle between the wooden benches. Over the *bima* the eternal light flickered. The ark where the Torah rested was surrounded by candles; some had melted. "The light isn't good here," Dina said. "I worry for my father's eyesight sometimes." She closed her eyes. "The great rabbi loses his sight but God gives him the power to recite the Torah from memory. All of it. He can open the scrolls and even though he cannot see, he knows his place, he can still inspire. Congregations from all over the world flock to this tiny synagogue to see him. To hear him. The word of God spills from his lips and he . . . he . . ."

They stood in the quiet for a moment and listened to the sounds of their breathing. After a moment Elie touched one finger to Dina's face, at the top of the bruise near her eye. He turned to the door, worried that someone might be watching. No one was there. He turned back. Dina's eyes remained fixed on Elie as he ran his finger across the patch of discolored skin. "Does it hurt?" he whispered.

"No. No. Not when you touch me."

He gently brushed away the hair that had fallen over her eyes. "Would you be angry with me — more angry with me — if I wanted to kiss you?"

"No one has ever wanted to kiss me before," she whispered. "Bernard would be angry at me if he knew you wanted to kiss me. So would Papa. Besides, no one has ever kissed me before. I don't really know how. Not like Lauren Bacall would anyway. You would be disappointed. I . . . would think I . . . Bernard would . . ." They moved together and she closed her eyes. As the light flickered behind them, they kissed.

MAY 1991

A few hours before dawn, I woke from a deep sleep and sat up, startled and confused by a terrifying dream. My room was still dark, though I could make out a line of light under the door. After a moment, I heard a medications cart roll by, accompanied by muffled conversation, punctuated by hearty laughter.

I was sweating; my bedclothes were stuck to my skin and my heart was beating so rapidly, it pulsated through my ears in the silence. Then, the dark images returned like feverish hallucinations: There was Sarah, her body being punctured by enormous blunt instruments, though no one held them. Then there was Sarah again, this time being strangled by a faceless assailant, a look of terror in her eyes. She reached out for me to help her, but I couldn't. Finally, Sarah's doctor, his face contorted in pure hatred, bore into me with fierce clarity.

The night's grim fare continued to assail me. The final reverie sent me reeling. Why was the doctor angry? Had I failed my wife in some way? I wondered whether the dream was an omen, but of what? Without a resolution, however, I eventually fell back into a heavy sleep.

When I woke again my clock read 9:30. Someone was pounding on my door.

"Are you okay, Mr. Gilman? I'm going to unlock the door," Belinda said.

"I'm fine," I yelled, "I'm sleeping, that's all."

There was a pause. "Are you sure? Is there anything I can do?"

"No, I'll be out later."

"Breakfast is over but we saved you a tray. Do you want me to bring it in?"

"No" I repeated, "I'll be out later."

Why did I have such terrible and confusing dreams, I wondered, and why was it that Sam Hersh's appearance and these nightmares arrived simultaneously? Had he been the catalyst? He was, after all, an annoyance. The others were equally idiosyncratic, and yet this was my first night filled with horrors.

I pulled back my blankets to look at my body. My legs were still different shapes, one thin and white and almost hairless, the foot off at an angle, the other thicker yet also undoubtedly withering. I folded my fingers into fists. They were more shriveled and bent than I remembered, except for the bulging and swollen joints. I studied my arms as well. Veins bubbled up through my skin, which lay like dough covering my bones, and where tendons had once protruded connecting my hands and my wrists, only patches of yellow pigment remained.

I turned to the mirror and studied the lines on my face. My eyes were still clear and green, but the skin around them had wrinkled, hanging in puffy lumps from my cheeks. White stubble surrounded my jowls, and even the skin that was free of whiskers was marked with age spots and redness. My hair was also nearly gone except for my eyebrows, which were a disheveled mess. Was this the same face that I saw when I looked in the mirror fifty, sixty, seventy years ago? I remembered my pictures as a child and it did not seem possible that I was the same person.

"Mr. Gilman! I am coming in." Belinda was back

"I'll dress and come to the porch."

"You will? I'll wait for you."

"I'll see you on the porch when I'm dressed." God help me, I thought.

I struggled to get dressed. The correct method was to brace my back against the wall while propping my bad knee up at an angle. This permitted me to slip my pant leg over the leaden foot and then tug the pants up to my thigh before putting in my other foot. Donning the sock was made simpler as the ends of my toes were within reach. Finally, when I had finished, I returned to my chair and pushed out into the hall.

To my relief, Belinda was not there. With trepidation, I headed toward the dining room.

I didn't have a watch, but I was sure that it was now about 10:30 and I would be reproached for expecting food before lunch was formally served. Convinced, however, that I was entitled to something more than the cold toast that had been saved for me at the nurses' station, I rolled on. They have my home, they can at least feed me when I am hungry. I reached the doorway.

"Abraham Gilman, isn't it?" someone asked behind me.

I half-turned a wheel until I could face the voice. The man was short, slight, and perfectly groomed. I did not recognize him.

"Who are you?"

"I'm David Green. Emunah's nutritionist." He spoke with pride, hoping, I gathered, that I should be impressed with his position or that I was grateful to be eating his meals. "You sit alone too much at meals, Mr. Gilman. Studies have shown that to be bad for your digestion. People eat too quickly when there are no interruptions for conversation."

He was the type that Sarah would have adored. He

was young, handsome, effusive, and he had a job that she would have deemed important. I was certain she would have considered him a doctor of sorts.

> *"I've seen every kind of doctor there is in the world," she lamented after she got sick.*
>
> *"Well we haven't seen Dr. Jones, he's a Doctor of Anthropology," I said, trying to cheer her up. "Or Doctor Ho, the dentist, he's a doctor of sorts. And come to think of it we haven't seen Dr. Alicia, the podiatrist we met a few years ago. Remember she called herself a doctor. And . . . "*
>
> *"If you say the word veterinarian," she interrupted me. "you will die before I do."*

"I'm a bit hungry," I said to David Green.

He smiled at me, then asked me to wait while he checked in the kitchen.

"Here's some wheat toast with margarine and marmalade — orange." He had reappeared. "The staff's very busy with lunch preparation. I had to fix this myself. This should get you through to lunch, which begins in about thirty minutes."

"I don't like marmalade." I turned my chair toward the door, "I'll eat later."

As I approached, I could hear an argument developing on the porch. Belinda's voice was unmistakable as she tried to calm her charges, but everyone seemed to be shouting at once. I stopped as I reached the entrance, wishing there was somewhere else I could go.

Resigned, I finally pushed myself into the room and prayed I would be inconspicuous.

"And what would be so terrible?" Maury said. He turned to Hersh. "If Maury likes the idea, of course it's no good. Why should it be so? Sam," he announced, "you should have such ideas every day!"

"I'm sorry, no," Belinda declared forcefully, scanning the room.

Nearly everyone was listening. Hannah Cohen, in particular, seemed interested. She had closed her book and drawn her blanket up to her waist. Her eyes followed Sam Hersh, who was pacing, albeit crookedly, between Belinda and the windows.

"It would be my pleasure to pay for the transportation," Hersh offered, glancing up at Belinda. "I had a business for over forty years, you'll remember. They have not taken it all yet."

"Such a kind offer," Gertie Nuestadt wheezed.

"A mitzvah," someone called from across the room.

"Go look for Mr. Brody, Belinda," a man near the television ordered. "You shouldn't be in charge of such decisions. It's not right that you can decide what can be done and what can't."

Only the card players at the table with Harry had not paused to take part in the debate.

"God should take me," Maury moaned. "I wish God would take me now."

A hail of protest showered on Maury for his dramatics and Belinda turned to leave. "I will discuss the matter with Mr. Brody," she said, though I was sure she was lying. "The answer will be the same, but I can ask."

She passed my chair. I reached down for my book. I was determined to show them I was above any petty nonsense, particularly if it was suggested by Hersh. My God, I thought in a panic, I've forgotten my book; it's back in my room. I can't sit here all day without something to discourage conversation. If I go back now, though, there'll be a fuss.

"Belinda," I said, in my most unctuous tone, before she reached the door.

"Abe," she said. "Cleaning up Washington Park. Is that what you want to do? Planting trees, as Mr. Hersh proposes, or scrubbing down graffiti on bridges? You'd like to participate?"

"I was going to ask you if you'd mind asking someone to get my book for me, on the night table, in my room. You're in no mood, however, to be asked favors. I am weary, but I'll get it myself." I made a slow movement with my hands toward the wheels, before looking up again. "By the way, I don't have any interest in this at all." I glared at Hersh.

"Oh, I'm sorry," Belinda responded, deflated. "Stay here, I'll have someone get your book."

An uneasy silence permeated the room. Several people looked at Hersh to find out what was next on his agenda. He shrugged, and continued his pacing, making wider turns to cover more ground as he acknowledged each one's sympathy.

I tried to avoid watching him, though it was difficult to look busy without my book. I kneaded my leg for a time and scratched at my cuticles after that. I'm not interested in your scrambled brains, I denounced him in my thoughts. When that nurse comes back with my book, I'll be relieved of this annoyance.

"A good idea you had, Sam. Mazel Tov," Maury blurted. Several others nodded. "A little help we can't get with such an idea — too much trouble — They hate Jews here. I've been telling this to you all along."

"I can't just sit," Hersh said to Hannah Cohen. "Every day for the past forty years I got up out of my bed and went to work. I ran my business for all that time. When I was sick, I went. When the weather was so terrible even the police would not go outside, I was at my register. Now I should sit?"

"Eh, enough already God dammit," Harry groused. "Just drop your Goddamn *tukhis* over there."

"Such kvetching," Gertie said, waving her fingers at him. "All the time kvetching. It is none of my business, of course, but you could just sit. It's not so terrible to rest. You give me *shpilkies* watching you walk back and forth. Why don't you sit with Hannah? The company would be good for you. For her too."

"From everything you get *shpilkies*," Maury sneered.

"Enough," Rose said. Several ladies around her murmured in agreement.

Hersh studied Hannah Cohen. "I think I need something to do, that's all. Is that so terrible?"

She smiled to show it wasn't at all terrible.

"Well," he declared with renewed vigor, "somewhere here there must be something to do, right?" He turned to stare at me, obviously wanting me to confirm that he'd likely find something to occupy his time.

"I'm going to read. It's quiet and you should try it." I turned my chair to face the doorway; waiting for my book. "You'd think she had to open the Red Sea to get here."

"Your grief, you wear like clothes," Rose Goodman said. "You worry me — we are good people here, Mr. Gilman."

For an instant I considered her criticism. Had my character flaws spoiled Sarah's happiness, somehow? Bristling, I decided they had not. I was the one, after all, who had been left alone, who had to witness her agonizing death and stand by helplessly, who was crippled because I had no one to watch over me.

"Those French girls will still want you after I'm gone," she whispered weakly on her last evening.

"Nobody wants seventy-five-year-old sad guys," I said, pushing back tears.

"I didn't mean that thing about embarrassing yourself."

"Well, it only took fifty years to get an apology, so I accept."

"All right," Maury said to Hersh. "So you want a job. You can work in the kitchen or the laundry downstairs. After all, what are you, Superman? You can suddenly throw down your cane and run around like some kind of a chicken?"

"You're right," Hersh sighed. "I'm just always nervous I'll be bored, that's all. It has been my affliction for as long as I remember."

"God forbid you should be bored," Maury continued more softly. "Maybe you should pack your bags and go to Florida, like everyone else. Or Israel. You can fight with the Arabs."

Sarah and I had taken a trip to the Middle East some years earlier and I remembered her awe, looking out over the desert where, miraculously, vegetables had grown.

"Every one of you men in our temple has to call an electrician to screw in a lightbulb," she said to me. "Look what these people can do."

"I can change a lightbulb."

"You haven't even figured out push-button phones yet. But your incompetence makes you cute. Honestly." She turned and rolled her eyes at our friends. "Christ the carpenter he will not be mistaken for."

Belinda was standing over me with my book in her hand. "I'm sorry," she said. "I'm tired today and it looked like a general mutiny had started. It seems to have quieted down. I shouldn't have accused you."

Hersh reached us, and gently took the book out of Belinda's hand. He looked at it as though he'd been hypnotized.

"My book you want now?" I said. "You may borrow it when I'm finished."

Hersh held the book up to his eyes and an odd expression came over him. He swiveled on his cane to face Hannah Cohen and held the book out to her. She stared at him mesmerized. "Can we do such a thing?" he asked.

Hannah Cohen considered his question. "It is very, very difficult."

"But it can be done?"

"Yes, perhaps."

"What's this book you're reading, Abe? From here with my eyes I can't see it," Maury interrupted. "How to become a cantor in three simple lessons? Can Maury know what is happening? Eh, why should anyone tell me? It is only Maury?"

Hersh handed the book back to me.

"Please don't waste your time," I said. "You have no idea of the effort. You're too old to start now. You don't have the skills."

"I have nothing but time, and help, I'll have plenty of anyway, right? Everyone here can help."

"Everyone talks in such circles," Gertie said, choking back a gravelly cough.

Maury tapped his knuckles on the table. "Now with that I agree. This is some kind of secret you're keeping? What is this book that gives Mr. Hersh ideas?"

Belinda shook her head. "I don't know."

"*Oye Gutenue,*" Maury whined. "Someone please let us know what's going on."

"Mr. Hersh is suggesting that he's going to write a

book," I said. "On what topic I have no idea . . . Actually, he's suggesting that you all help him write a book. That is, if I'm understanding you correctly."

"Oh, fer chrissakes, please," Harry said coarsely, dropping his cards on the table. "Sam, take a pill or something. Every day it's something new with you. We can't even play over here." He glared at the man next to him. "Do you see this card? What are you, a moron? You're ruining my Goddamn game, Sam." He looked toward the staff station. "Do you people see what's going on here?" He pointed at Hersh. "Son of a bitch."

I considered telling Hersh that I had tried many times to do exactly what he was proposing and that each time the enormity of the task had overwhelmed me. I also thought I might emphasize my point by telling him that even with the impetus of my lifelong desire to be a writer, I had no success. I said nothing.

"With the cards put down, Harry, just like that, you can help me," Hersh said. "We can all put our *keppeles* together."

"We all hold one pencil?" Maury asked. "How could such a thing work?"

"You have somewhere else to go?" Hersh asked. "Something so important to do? Why not try this. We don't have to go anywhere. Your health, it can't hurt. All we need is patience. We can work right here. On the porch."

"How would we do it?" Rose asked.

Hersh mumbled. He appeared to realize that he didn't know.

"It can't be done." I said, breaking the silence. "Writing is personal. You do it or you don't do it. It's not susceptible to collaboration. If you want to write, sit down and write. Leave the rest of us to ourselves."

Hersh turned to me. "You were a teacher, no? You

could help us. What did you teach? You told me, but my memory is not so good."

"I didn't."

"Such a coincidence, you were a teacher?"

Maury interupted, "I was a teacher. Eighth grade at the Hillel School for thirty-four years, yet." He looked proud of his record.

"What subject did you teach, Abe?" Hannah Cohen asked.

"English — the public schools."

"And from where do you get such assurance that we can't do this?" Rose Goodman asked.

I had no answer though I was sure such a project could never be completed. I knew the intricacies of written composition and had read many histories of the heartbreak and trauma that afflicts aspiring writers. This was neither the time of life to start writing nor the team that could do it. And even if they were capable, Hersh clearly had no discernible ability to lead them.

Hersh pounded his cane on the floor in defiance. "Why this is so difficult to consider, I have no idea. All we do here is sit. You sit. I sit. Maury sits. What great burden would this be to try? What great tradition or rule would we break by scratching some words on paper?" He rested. Shock blanched the faces staring at him. "If I'm shouting, I'm sorry. I don't know why we couldn't all put together our heads and come up with an idea or two — writing, correcting — everyone could have a say, we could all have our say. Everyone helps, everyone talks, that's all." He scanned the room. "If it works, Mazel Tov to us. If not, then not."

"This won't work," I said. "Impossible. You're just begging these people to stand in line for a taste of disappointment."

"And, what would we write about?" Maury inquired.

"That, I can't answer," Hersh acknowledged. "That

we would have to decide together. Whatever it is, we'll be careful. Everyone will have a say. It will be like a minyan at shul. Without agreement, nothing. Not a word will be written."

"Such a thing is foolish," I said, aware of how loudly I was speaking. "Is there anyone here who has ever written anything? Anything more than a postcard? Who here can punctuate? Type? And how do you think up a book by committee? Enough already. Just go about your business. This writing, it's work. Hard work."

"Typing, I can do," someone said. "I can type," she repeated proudly.

"Hersh, you and I, we'll do it," Maury said. "How much work can it be?"

Hersh did not seem pleased with Maury's support.

"So, we'll try it," a man near Harry said, pushing his chair back from the card table.

"Eh, fer chrissakes," Harry yelled, "sit down."

"Hersh has an idea. Why is it so terrible to help him?" He was, without question, waiting for instructions, the inevitable occurring much sooner than I expected, I thought smugly.

"Just go back and play cards," I implored.

Rose Goodman struggled to rise out of her chair. She straightened slowly, and when she was up, she took a deep breath, as if to draw us all into her lungs. "I can also type, when my fingers aren't stiff like branches. I'll help you, Mr. Hersh."

He turned then, to Hannah Cohen.

"I was an editor at the *Jewish Advocate* for twenty-five years," she said.

"The newspaper? For twenty-five years?"

"Yes, I think I can help you."

FEBRUARY 1948

Growing up, Elie often wondered how it was possible that he could honor his parents as the Torah and the Talmud required. Being giving and helpful to his mother, as his teachers at the Yeshiva had instructed him, was easy. But how could he acknowledge a man for whom he had only the faintest of recollections?

"How do I honor my father?" he remembered asking, Rabbi Chymer. "I only know him from his picture and from my imagination."

"You say the Kaddish, and maintain your memories, whatever they are, even across the passing of time."

Elie decided, then, to think of his father once each day, before bed. For many nights afterward he lay awake and wondered what his father was like, and imagined how brave he was in the face of death at the hands of the Nazis.

Elie turned off Blue Hill Avenue and walked down Babson Street past the darkened row houses on both sides, set just back from the sidewalk. When he reached the corner of Crossman Street, he climbed the narrow stairs leading to the second-floor tenement just above where Isidore Krupp and his ailing wife, Edith, the landlords, resided.

"I'm home. Are you okay?"

His mother lay on the couch, listening to the radio, as she did at the end of each day.

"I'm making you some tea."

"Eat first. I can wait. You keep such hours, I'm worried for you."

"What are you listening to?" he called from the kitchen.

"Reports on Palestine. Such terrible fighting. I'm wondering how many people from Freiburg are there. How many people from Shaary Tefila." Elie knew this was the synagogue her family had attended when she was a girl. "People they must get tired of fighting day after day. It's difficult. Very difficult. Many must give up."

Elie weighed his mother's words. "Do you think Papa's there?"

"Mrs. Shetzel, she's telling me on the telephone that you're visiting with Rebbe Kishenev. She's saying that you have been visiting with Dina Kishenev." Elie understood that she was changing the subject. "Dina Kishenev, she's to be married to the son of Rebbe Liebenshul."

"I hit her in the face with a basketball. It was an accident. I just went to make sure she was all right." He set the tea on the end table.

"I heard this. And the game lost too," she said. "Please, no worrying about this. Walking and reading at the same time Mrs. Shetzel says. This is what she does, Dina Kishenev."

"I was just checking on her."

"Let her be married to the rebbe's son. The shuls need this to be. You are . . ." she searched for the right word. "You are mixing up this sorriness you feel."

Elie realized that the years had worn heavily on his mother.

"She's a nice girl. Mrs. Shetzel should mind her own business."

"Mrs. Shetzel, she's a good friend. You should be nice," his mother said. "She likes the gossip. People like many worse things."

"Do you think Papa might be in Palestine?" He was nervous to ask her, but the rebbe's words nagged at him. "There are thousands of people from Europe there and we never do really talk about what happened to him after we left Freiburg. Do you think he could be there?"

"I'm too tired to talk of such things now. I'm going to bed."

"Wait, wait" Elie said. He squeezed her hand. "I want to tell you what Rabbi Kishenev told me tonight. It's important that you know."

"I don't want to talk now," his mother begged. "Please."

"Listen just for one minute. He told me there's an organization, a service that helps people locate those from Europe. People who were lost during the war. They have records, he said. They can help us."

"What can they help us to do?"

He wanted to tell his mother every detail of his visit with the Kishenevs, to explain that the rabbi too had suspicions about the reasons for Elie's appearance there. More than that, he wanted his mother to know that Mrs. Kishenev was worried Bernard Liebenshul could not make Dina happy; that she thought he was uncaring. He wanted her to know more about Dina; about how they looked at one another, and how certain he was that he could tell Dina anything. But he wouldn't tell her. He wanted her to hear what the rabbi had said about resolving her husband's destiny. That he would say.

The tintype of Elie's father was faded and yellowing. He could recall every detail from memory. He handed the picture to his mother. "I know that you were married. I know that he was a reporter for the *Abenpost* in Freiburg.

I know he fought in the First War and that he did many brave things — *Der Hebraisch Held,* I've heard that name. I know something also about the boycotts, and I know that he stayed behind to help." His mother, in pain, shut her eyes. "That's all I know. Those are the only things I know about my father.

"I don't have many memories. I don't know if he ever played with me, kissed my forehead, talked to me; I don't remember him hugging us, ever being with us, being with you, lighting the candles, reading to me, going to the synagogue on the Sabbath. I don't remember any of that." He waited for a response, but she remained quiet. "The strangest part is, though, I know that I want to be just like him. I need to know everything about him. He was my father. I need to hear everything about him."

He could see she would not speak.

"Do you know what happened to him? So much time has passed. Are you thinking that it's possible that he's in Israel? I can understand it if you think that. There are so many there and it's been so long." Elie wanted to shout at her. He wanted to scream his frustration at God for not having his father. "Mama, I don't think it is possible that Papa survived. I . . . I don't . . . I think he died somewhere maybe in Germany. He died, I think. We have to face it. He isn't in Israel. We would have heard from him by now."

"No," she said curtly. "No. No. This, I would know. No. I can still feel him. Here he is, inside me."

"I have been trying to find out what happened to him," Elie admitted. "I wasn't going to tell you until I learned something. I don't know much, yet. I've gone to the army and to the consulates."

"I think it's easier not to know," she whispered. Her eyes filled. "Please."

"Honor your mother and father, Rabbi Kishenev told me. Honoring your parents is more important than even honoring God. He said that I do Papa no honor and that I do you no benefit by waiting for these answers. He's right. I want to find out what happened to him. I need to find out what happened. And so do you."

"Elie, it is easier on my heart if I don't know, and if I don't talk of him. Every night I go to my bed and I dream that the next day — I pray that the next day — will be when he comes to us. I can sleep at night because I have this hope. If I know he's gone, then I have no more hope, and no more sleep. I need to have my hope, my Elie. Is this too much?"

Elie wondered how many others after the war were left like his mother. How many sat at their windows, waiting. He realized he was one of those people; that the feeling he had known from childhood, which he could not identify until now, was loneliness.

"When you're ready — sometime — I want you to tell me more about him," Elie said. "We don't have to talk about the sad things, Mama. Or the war. And not even today. But sometime I'd just like to hear more about him. Just anything that comes to mind. If he's alive, speaking of him won't change it. I promise."

"I know that somewhere he's looking and searching for us; for you and for me. He loves you so much. Sometimes I have the feeling he's close. Around the corner perhaps, near."

Elie was exasperated and tired. "It's okay," he said. "Not tonight. Maybe tomorrow you can tell me more."

He wanted his mother to go on, but knew she was devastated by the prospect that her husband was gone. They both fell back against the blanket thrown over the sofa.

"The rabbi's daughter, she's a nice girl? A heart like gold, Mrs. Shetzel is telling me." Elie could see she was nervous. "When you are speaking of her, I can see your father in your face."

Elie did not want to address her concerns about Dina. He was frustrated. "We'll talk later. You're tired. I shouldn't have confronted you with this tonight. I'm sorry. Rabbi Kishenev, he —"

"It's all right," she said. "He's right. You should know, and I should be telling you these things." She leaned forward and placed her palm on his cheek. "You like this girl?"

Elie was torn. He wanted her to know how he felt, but he wanted to protect Dina as well. "She's concerned about helping the rebbe. He wants his congregation and the Khal Anshei Chessed to be brought together. He's worried that if they stay divided they will be weaker. Everyone is concerned about what happened . . ." Elie hesitated. "in the camps."

"Yes," his mother responded. "Yes, I know. Mrs. Shetzel, she tells me this Bernard is a very serious boy. A scholar, she says."

"That's what everyone says. I don't know, we've never met," Elie said.

He turned to his mother whose eyes were closed. She was clearly flooded with memories. She began to cry.

"It's late," Elie said. "You have work tomorrow."

She stood, and wiped her face, first with her hands, then her sleeves.

"Rabbi Kishenev, he's a good man, yes?"

"The whole family is very nice. I wish you could meet them."

"Someday — Someday."

"It's okay," Elie hugged her.

She pushed away. "You should know. You should know. I'm sorry."

"I want to know," Elie said, "but only when you're ready to tell me. I don't need to hear it tonight."

Lena Wasserman shook her head. "I will tell you. I promise. I will."

Elie watched her shift and grow uncomfortable. "I will. I will." She trembled and seemed to go limp. "But first, there is a man here. Here in Mattapan. He can tell you things. He can tell you about the war. About the name *Der Hebraisch Held*. He was with your father during the First War. Go to him. These are things you should hear from your father, not a stranger. But, now, go to him."

Elie was stunned and angry.

"This man, he lives near the movie house. In the Square. His name is Menachem Kultz. He lives at the number fifty-two. Up the stairs. He is also from Freiburg."

"You never mentioned him before. Why not?"

"I go to see him. Not often. Not often, but I go. More than that I just cannot do. Visit him. He can tell you what you want to hear."

Elie sat alone in the dark. His life, it seemed, was full of secrets. The fate of his father. His feelings for Dina. The service run by Frana Luftwantz. And now this man, Menachem Kultz. He felt lost.

I need you, he thought, imagining Dina's face.

He tried to remember Freiburg. Did I run and play? Did old ladies grab my cheeks and pinch me? What did our house look like? Who were our neighbors?

He tried to imagine the face of Menachem Kultz. Who was he? Why was he unknown to him?

He thought of Bernard then, and felt sorry for him.

"I wish I could help you," he said aloud. "I don't know you, and you don't even know you need it, but I wish I could help you."

JUNE 1991

Visitors were welcome at Emunah and several came on a regular basis. Harry's son, Saul, came on Tuesdays, usually followed by Maury's three grandchildren, dragged behind their mother. Dr. Nathan also had visitors, though they appeared to be former patients rather than offspring, and perhaps most noteworthy, Belinda's cousin, Elbert the Magician, arrived to make a charitable contribution of his talents, though his beneficiaries — myself in particular — found him tiresome.

I had no visitors at all. Artie and Elaine Stern, a couple we had known for many decades, had moved to a far-off locale called Citrus Village, in Castabula, Florida, and Sid Naiman, my best friend for as long as I could remember, had died of cancer five years earlier. Sarah's brother, Arthur, my only remaining in-law, had failed to appear at the Shiva or to contact me after the accident, and even Maxwell Brody, who had come to my room twice during my first week at Emunah to check on my progress, never came again after I was less than effusive.

Mail was also unlikely, so, though I passed by my assigned box every day, I neglected to even check for correspondence. Despite my lack of interest, I was, the day after Hersh announced his plan to author a book, amazed to receive two written communiqués. I had not, as usual, made the trip to my box, but Maury, having noticed the letters, dropped them on my tray at lunch.

The letters were noteworthy, both for their content and because their writers were people with whom I had little contact. The first was from Jennifer Kent and was typed on stationery emblazoned with her firm's name: LEGAL SERVICES FOR THE ELDERLY, COUNSELORS AT LAW.

May 14, 1991

Dear Mr. Gilman,

I would like to take this opportunity to thank you for your cooperation at our earlier meeting, and I believe I can express the appreciation of Mr. Brody as well. This process is sometimes difficult to understand and accept and while you were quite properly surprised to find your options limited, you handled yourself like a gentleman and with much respect. You should know that my position as an attorney for Legal Services for the Elderly (LSE) requires that I retain contact with those patients I have aided and that I must continue to monitor their progress whether they return home or whether they move onto one of the fine institutions available, such as the Emunah Retirement Home and Convalescent Center.

In that regard, it is my understanding that your transition has been somewhat difficult. Mr. Brody, in his report to the Department of Social Services (DSS) for the month of January, reports that you continue to display some reticence to socialize with the other residents and that you have been less than cooperative with some of the staff.

I am writing you this letter to express both my surprise at this report as well as to inform you of the current status of the funds available for your care.

First, please be advised that it is my responsibility, when I learn of patients undergoing difficult transitions, to investigate that potential for continued difficulties and to make recommendations as to possible care alternatives. While this drastic action is not currently required, I have made preliminary inquiries in an effort to determine the probable reasons for your reluctance to find comfort at Emunah.

I have learned from Dr. Glick, your primary care physician, that prior to the death of your wife, you were known widely as an amicable man of "high moral principles" and that you had a long prosperous marriage. It is also Dr. Glick's opinion that your current difficulties are the direct result of the extended mourning period that often accompanies the death of a spouse. (I understand also that your wife was a remarkable, charitable woman and that she is missed by many, including much of the staff at the hospital, who truly found her an enjoyable personality).

Regardless of your respectable past attributes, please accept this correspondence as notice to you that the DSS has requested that they be permitted to make further investigation into your case and that as a result of that investigation, that they be permitted to supplement their prior recommendations.

I stopped reading, and I tore up the letter. How dare Jennifer Kent scold me for my behavior. How could she, without my permission, still conduct interrogations of my doctors and examine my personal records? Most vexing was the insinuation that her rekindling of the memory of Sarah was somehow going to transform me; as if I simply needed a reminder of Sarah's good nature, which, once received, would forever reorder my personality. I considered asking her to withdraw from my case and never to interfere again. I was not disruptive, anyway, I convinced myself — I simply wanted to be left alone — and anyone who felt otherwise was simply overstating the facts.

The second correspondence was a condolence letter, of sorts. It was postmarked from Philadelphia, and was dated December 10, 1990, leading me to wonder about the route it must have taken before finally arriving in my box. There was also the possibility that it had sat at Emunah unnoticed for several weeks, but I concluded that Maury was far too concerned with my affairs to have allowed such a delay.

Dear Abraham,

You and I did not know each other well, but I feel like I must write to you to tell you how saddened I am over Sarah's passing. I am sorry it has taken me so long to write to you.

Sarah was a very special person in my life always. I don't know of any other person who made me feel so special and so loved. She was as beautiful on the inside as she was outside, much more beautiful than I. It is just not often that people go through your life who give the kind of joy Sarah did. Everyone was touched by her and she had a power to bring cheer to the world.

I am writing this letter to you also to confess in a way. I do not know whether Sarah explained this to you, but during her visit here many years ago, in July of 1967, during my husband's illness, without asking or telling me, she paid all of our household bills that had piled up for several months.

I do not have any idea of the amount of money she spent and was so sad and scared then that I did not understand she had done this for a long time. Jeremy, my husband, died soon after that and I was never able to repay you, and I was too ashamed to tell Sarah that I knew she had done this for me. Anyway, many many years too late I thank you for your part in this kindness. I know you were not wealthy then and this was a great sacrifice for you too.

I hope you are getting along well. It is very difficult to lose your husband or wife.

With much sadness, I am
Elaine Socholitzky

Sarah had, on a number of occasions, undertaken to quietly relieve financial strain on our friends or relatives; strain usually caused by catastrophe, and had always done so secretly. Nonetheless, I searched my memory for some recollection of this particular grant and could find none.

I sat inert and depressed until an orderly approached me. I nudged my tray in his direction so he would take it, even though I had eaten nothing. A half hour later, leaving the letters behind, I maneuvered my chair back into the hall.

"Okay, So there is this guy," Harry said, as I pushed onto the porch. "This Mr. McCallister. He is riding a train, the

Broadway, from New York to Chicago. Anyways he's gonna make a little speech when he gets there and well, of course he's a little nervous so he decides he wants to get some sleep, and just as he's about to go out he hears this yenta's voice behind him. 'Oye,' she moans, 'am I toisty.' Harry exaggerated a Yiddish inflection and a woman's voice. "Well, this Mr. McCallister, he tries to ignore the lady, and begins to drift off again, when of course she starts in again. 'Oye am I toisty, Oye am I toisty.' Well, now he's getting a little annoyed, a little mad now, after all he's got to make this big talk the next day, but still he decides to ignore it. Well, a few minutes pass and she's back, 'Oye, am I toisty.' " Harry made a rolling motion with his hands "Now, Mr. McCallister is really not happy, and he starts to think: What can I do? Well, he decides he can either yell at her or he can be a mensch and go get her a cup of water. He's a nice guy, so he figures he'll get the water, and he runs down to the end of the car and gets the lady a water." Harry shrugged as if to say he would not have made that choice. "Anyway, he walks back and hands the lady her water and he says 'this will take care of you and then we can both get some sleep.' "

I looked over at Hersh, who rubbed his eyes, and at Hannah Cohen who seemed to be enthralled. "This yenta lady, she tells him thank you, drinks up the water. and McCallister gets back into his seat and starts to drift off to sleep, happy he could fix the problem. Then just as he's about to be sleeping, she moans: 'Oye vas I toisty. Oye vas I toisty.' "

Several people around the table chuckled politely. What they had heard was obviously not what Hersh had envisioned when he asked everyone to participate. Nevertheless, Harry seemed heartened that he had drawn some snickering.

"Your jokes are not so funny," Maury said.

"Bachhh. Here's another one," he said defiantly. "This horse, he is having a bad day, so he goes to shul to see the rabbi —"

I stopped listening and turned to watch Hersh instead. He remained calm and even smiled at Harry's effort, but I suspected he was doing only what he thought best to keep the group moving.

"Abe?" Hersh said. "What do you think?" He pointed at a set of tables aligned in the center of the room. His volunteers had already joined him. "Here, we can work. Everyone is going to tell a story and we will pick one to write down."

"Such hard work you will never know," I said loud enough for everyone to hear. "You'll all have passed on before you could finish such a thing. With God's help we'll all be gone soon anyway."

"Abe, we're not begging."

"A cure this is not. You'll all still be old and sick, even if you put words on paper."

"Some wonderful suggestions already we've had," Hersh continued, ignoring me. He lifted his hand and spread his short, knobby fingers in front of his face. "Harry, he thinks a book of comedy would be good for us to do." He began to check off ideas by curling his fingers, one by one, into his fist. "And Mel," he gestured to one of Harry's friends, "he told a story of how he clopped a girl spectator on the nose with a bad shot at a basketball game at the JY and then ended up marrying her." Another finger folded into his palm. He held his accounting in place with the other hand. "Rachel here, *kena hora,*" he pointed to a woman sitting nervously at the far end of the table, "about her father, the famous Polish writer who was killed for whisking Jews to safety away from the Nazis in the middle of the night"

"I will give my account now," Rose Goodman said. "God should give me strength." She reached for her walker and wrung her fingers tightly around the top metal bar. "I — I am not a married woman. I have never been married."

No one seemed surprised by this revelation; her domineering nature, at least to me, not being wholly suited to the institution of marriage anyway. Nevertheless, she examined her listeners to determine whether she would be criticized for lying or ostracized for going her entire life without a mate. Though most of the expressions around her showed indifference, it was clear that her status as a spinster was of great concern to her.

"This was not a terrible thing for me," she went on. "No one has been in love with me, and my responsibilities, well, they've kept me from marriage. I am not troubled by this. I don't expect sympathy —"

"I'm not married either," said Belinda. "It's okay, really. I don't think anyone really minds you said you weren't."

"It's not a surprise," Maury muttered from the sofa.

"To begin," Rose said, "I'll tell you that as a girl, my father had a store. My father he sold trinkets, a book here on this shelf, and over there handkerchiefs, nothing really, but at night he studied Talmud, so it did not matter. God willing, if someone came in, a sale was made."

She shifted in her chair, using her walker to brace herself. "For endless hours my father studied there. And every morning he prayed at Beth Abr. Some of you may remember this shul. It's gone now."

She moistened her lips with her tongue. "Anyway, when the war came, and the Germans with their camps and their factories for killing, my father pleaded with God, and he looked at the Talmud for answers; why this would happen to the Jews? In the shul, the rebbe, he told my father and the others to pray for the killing to stop. He said he had no answers as to why this would happen to us."

"She's married?" Gertie growled. "She's not married? What? I can't hear. There was a wedding? Was there a wedding? Can we talk in a voice I can hear?"

There was little about my own wedding day that I recalled vividly. The flowers and decorations were a blur, the rabbi nondescript, the ceremony a cacophony of words. I had no stories to reminisce about involving miraculous last minute arrivals at the sanctuary by the best man or acts of God causing the electricity to falter, guests to faint, or the chupa to fall at our feet. But Sarah's face that day! She was so beautiful I wanted to cry with joy — fall into tears at my good fortune. Her eyes were wide and full of wonder; her perfect smile told me she was happy.

Rose woke me from my daydream. "How do we stop this? How can we keep this from happening again to us? The likes of Hitler will come again. How do we prepare ourselves for this? Some of you may remember there was fear. Great fear.

"Some in the congregation, they said that we shouldn't be so different, shouldn't keep to ourselves so much. That this is what makes them suspicious of us. They said we should take off our black coats and yarmulkes. That the men should shave off their beards and earlocks. They said that we should throw out tradition, make ourselves more modern. Make it so that we look like them!" She shuddered. "These people, they wanted us to hide. To forget our ways. My father to stop studying Talmud.

"Others, they had different ideas. Join the shuls together, they said. We must speak with one voice; be of one heart. If we are together, we will be stronger. The hand is stronger with the fingers folded together." She made a fist. "And weaker when they're wide and apart from one another." Her hand opened slowly. "There were seven, or perhaps eight other shuls, Ba'ale Batim, Congregation Khal Adath Yeshuren, Chizuk Amuna, others. Some of the rebbes agreed, others said no."

I stopped paying attention. Maybe something dreadful had happened to Sarah's brother. Well, even so, there was nothing I could do. I concerned myself, next, with Sarah's grave and its upkeep, then the bleak condition of my leg. What if other painful accidents occurred? And though I was adroit at repressing most of these concerns, the one thought that I could not dismiss was that other people — strangers — were living in my house, occupying rooms where my life once had prospered. In a whirl of recollections, I roamed from room to room, reviewing the belongings and furniture I had left behind. The sensation I was left with was a mixture of terror and emptiness; it was as if I had been robbed, and violated, or had lost everything in a terrible hurricane or fire. There was a swell of bitterness in my throat. I realized how tragic my existence had become.

By the time I refocused, Rose was finished, and Maury, though clearly no one cared, commenced his pitiful saga of a mugging he endured outside the synagogue a year before arriving at Emunah.

"If they would have asked first, I would have given them the money," he cried.

"My contribution isn't really a story at all," Hannah Cohen said. "I'd just like to tell you about a friend with whom I grew up and who meant a great deal to me. I'm sorry. It may not be that exciting. I just wish everyone had known her. She was very special. She deserves to be remembered by me, that's all. I miss her."

Hersh was clearly enthralled. He gazed up as if to thank God for the privilege of hearing Hannah Cohen. "You are like Einstein. What a mind you have."

Despite my better intentions, I too, felt compelled to

hear her. It wasn't surprising that it was Hannah Cohen who brought something fresh to these dreary proceedings.

"We were inseparable. My mother used to say to her: 'Don't ever change. Don't ever change,' she would say when she saw her."

She rested her trembling hands on the table.

"Her name was Bea, Bea Sondelman."

"No," a man said, leaning forward. "Bea Sondelman, who lived downstairs from the Crossmans? On Wellington Street?"

"Yes." Hannah Cohen responded with delight and surprise. "Did you know her?"

"I knew Axel Crossman. Do you remember Axel Crossman, Harry? He played basketball with Joel Mochiber at Hecht House. Do you remember?" He frowned. "I think Axel passed away. Did Axel pass away, Harry?"

"Mrs. Cohen should finish before we start in," Hersh suggested.

"She talked in daydreams." the man recalled. "That I remember."

"Yes, that's right. She did," Hannah said.

"Someone should explain this to me," Hersh requested. "How do you talk in daydreams? This, I don't understand."

Hannah smiled. "Her imagination — you always knew what was in her imagination — because she told you. If you told her your father was mad at you, she would make up a story: 'perhaps you will be banished from the house and end up in a terrible orphanage, only to become famous as a ballerina,' she would say, 'And then upon your return to an adoring crowd, your father will come and beg your forgiveness.' I remember once Hasada Pakarski dropped a cholly bread at the Sabbath dinner and she came to the Temple in tears. Her mother was angry. Anyway, Bea starts in that she would be expelled from the home and then exiled back to Europe, only to be a stowaway on a freighter, and to come back to her mother who would be so worried she would be tearing her clothes. Being exiled was one of her favorites.

"It was from books that she took these stories. More than anything else she loved to read. All day long and into the night she would read. While she walked, she would read.

"She would get so lost in a book that she would be practically in a trance. You could talk to her, walk by her, wave your hands at her and she wouldn't be disturbed. You had to shake her almost to get her back. And then she would apologize, she just didn't know that she was doing it, and she would become embarrassed, especially if it was my mother or Zeda who was trying to speak to her. We'd be nervous sometimes because she'd take a book with her on the way home, and my mother was sure someone would knock her over or that a bus would crash into her on the street because she was not watching where she was going."

"Fer Chrissakes," Harry spit out with frustration. "People are nice. People like to read books, fer Chrissakes. Abe may be a crackpot, but he's right. We don't know the first thing about this book writing."

"A little help then, he could give us; it might be good," Maury glanced at me.

"You shouldn't keep asking. My mind's made up." I rolled my chair back a full turn, hoping my retreat would discourage more questions. It would have been perfect justice, I thought then, not to have answered while I was allegedly reading — just as Bea Sondelman would have done.

"Who hasn't gone?" Hersh inquired

"Me," a woman cried out. She had never said anything before, and as with many of the patients, I'd made no effort to learn her name. "But with such a group of kvetchers, maybe I should wait. Who can listen with all this *mishigas*?"

"Thelma Singer!" Hersh said surprised. "Go ahead. The noise has stopped."

"I thank you very much for taking such precious time to listen," Thelma said. "Many years ago in Poland, the Russians, they were in charge." She made a motion as if she were spitting to the side of her chair. "These Russians you know, they were every bit as bad in their day for the Jews as was our friend Mr. Hitler. Jews were beaten and killed then just as always. You need somebody to hate; take the Jews; everybody else does. Anyway, this miserable Russian army, they come to the ghetto where the Jews live, all in peace and nice I should add, and the rabbi, of course, he looks after this town of nice, peaceful people. Well, the leader of this army of *chazzeri* comes to the town and, like all the others, he's a dirty anti-Semite. He goes up to the rabbi and he says that everyone in the town should leave their homes and come to the square in the center of the town. The rabbi, who doesn't want any trouble, he says okay.

"So they all gather at the square and this mumzer he says to the rabbi, if your God is so great, let's see if he can help you today. Then he takes off his hat. Here is my hat, he says to the rabbi. I've got two papers inside folded at the bottom. One says the word life, the other says the word death. You pick one. If it says life, your people can live and they can go home; if it says death, I will kill them all right here."

She paused. Several people gestured for her to continue. "Well, the rabbi, he's with the *yiddisha kopf* like I say." She tapped on her temple. "He knows a filthy liar when he sees one, so he knows death is written on both slips. He thinks for a minute, and then, he reaches in, and before they can stop him he puts the paper in his mouth, swallows it, and takes a beating from the anti-Semite. 'How am I to tell which slip you've chosen?' the *chazzer* says to the rabbi. And the rabbi says to him, you just look at the slip still in the hat and whatever it says I picked the other one."

"I — I would not say these were stories you telling us."

The silence was broken not by Hersh or Hannah Cohen or by anyone else I recognized, but by an unfamiliar voice. Along with everyone else, I looked for the source of the comment. It was a woman in a wheelchair pushed off to one side. Until this moment I had never seen her awake.

"Stories — no — no," she repeated. I noticed how thin she was, her skin was nearly transparent. Her hands were gnarled into a fist and she held tightly to a tissue. Her eyes, which were open for the first time that I could recall, were cloudy and bloodshot. I thought about my own colorless flesh, and the deadened nerves and muscles in my own leg, and felt a moment of panic.

"Do you have something you want to tell us, Mrs. Silver?" Belinda inquired. "We'll listen if you want to speak."

"Our name is not Silver." She spoke haltingly, but not, it seemed, to emphasize her point, but because she was uncomfortable with English and wanted to choose her words carefully. "The name became changing when we come to New York." It was difficult to hear her until Belinda moved her wheelchair closer. I guessed her to be over ninety, though I was a terrible judge of age. "Schem," she said and nodded to no one. "Our name then was Schem, Albert and Edelin Schem." Harry complained that he couldn't hear. "Forgive me, please, I am speaking still with poor words, but Albert and I, we are coming from Freiburg, this is in Germany. I live as a child in Freiburg and Avi my son, he was born there, also. Before the war, the boat coming to take us. We arriving here then."

"What did she say?" Harry said to Hersh. He didn't answer.

"My Albert, he did not come with the boat. We are

begging him to come. We are begging to him. He would not come on the boat.

"I am screaming at him as the boat pulling away. *Verpflegen, verpflegen, verpflegen,* I am screaming. But he wait there on the shore and we go, Avi and I, alone without a husband. Avi without a father."

Around the table, people were straining to hear her. I labored to listen also.

Belinda handed her a new tissue. "Thank you. My remembering is not so good. I am even forgetting sometimes what I am holding." She shut her eyes. "God, he should be taking me now. I am old. I am ready."

"This isn't necessary, Mrs. Silver," Belinda said. "There's time."

"Worrying. All the time, darling, you worrying. There is nothing else for such an old woman. Wait. Fine, I am, all fine." She smiled. "My Albert, he is proud to be German. Before the First War, the Jews, you see, they were welcome to be in Germany. Before the First War, the Jews were inside the government, and inside the business, and doctors and anything at all." I tried to pinpoint the setting — sometime in the early 1900s, I guessed. "Anything. But the Jews with this welcoming had also to be fighting, to be soldiers. Wanting to be fighting in the war. So my Albert, he join with the army, and off he is going, to fight the British and the French and the other enemies.

"Many letters, I am getting from Albert from this war. He is telling me of the battles, and how terrible, and of the fighting and the killing. And when the holidays are coming he would write how he could not be lighting the candles for Chanukah or for the Sabbath. And that soon home he would be coming. The end of the war was coming soon. Saying this in the letters.

"Help me with my straightening, please, darling," she said to Belinda.

"Then the war is finishing," she said abruptly.

She looked up. It was not difficult, at that moment, to understand that this was not a story she told often.

"And finally —" She wiped her eyes. "Oh, it was a day of such happiness. This man he is a good man and he is my husband. I am proud and so happy. And, of course, many others from the town also coming home, but, well they all, they are speaking of Albert and how brave. Many mothers come to him and they kissing his *keppele* for their children that he save. The stories they are telling in many places. Even the goyim soldiers telling stories of Albert, they are calling him *Der Hebraisch Held,* telling me on the street that Albert saving this one or another one. Protecting them. *Der Hebraisch Held, Der Hebraisch Held.* Saying this in the street. They are calling to him."

"Maybe that will be enough for today, Mrs. Silver?" Belinda said. "Could we pick this up tomorrow? We can start right here. No interruptions."

"Shh," Maury said, then apparently reconsidered. He fell back into his chair.

"Mrs. Silver, do you want to stop? Hersh said. "I want to hear more, but, if you're tired —"

"Let me go on, darling. It is all right."

Everyone in the room was watching her, fascinated.

"This was a happy time for us, before the terrible Depression beginning. No, we are not the most wealthiest people. Albert, he is not the genius for the money, he is typing for the job, but he is a good man, the best kind of man, kind to me and to Avi, going to the shul on the Sabbath. Working. We are having the food and we are having a good family. What else do we need?

"Then coming the Nazis," Mrs. Silver whispered. "From nothing we know of suffering until they coming to the government. Nothing. They say changes they will be making. There will be no more starving they say, because the people who have made Germany to be weak will have no more power. And, of course, it is the Jews the Nazis are saying are making Germany to be no good. Well, when this is all you are hearing this is what you are believing. They are teaching this hatred to the children in the schools. The Jewish bankers, they are stealing all the money from Germany, the good jobs and the good businesses, owned by the Jews. The Jews are criminals and dirty. Albert, he is not believing what is happening. At the newspaper where is his job, he is telling everyone this, that these terrible things they are not the truth. One day I am hearing him talking to Juergen Burghardt, also who working at the *Abenpost*. Albert saying to him, am I so rich? Am I causing food not to be on the table? I was a soldier. Fighting so hard for this country. But Juergen he is saying why would they be saying such things if they are not the truth? There are so many problems he is saying, these are only happening when the Jews are having all the money."

She leaned forward. "Soon, into the jails, fuff, like this." She waved the back of her hand. "On the streets, there is terror. Dark men with such eyes as to be killing with just looking, these men wandering the streets for nothing but to be burning and killing. Shops, homes, schools, and synagogues, synagogues blazing with fire, burning and burning, and people running in and out, scared, oye, shaking with such frightening. Avi is crying always, and I also am, and then more windows breaking on the ground, and more fire, and people with blood on the hands and the faces, or lying in the street the heads opening for the blood to be running out.

"Well, I am saying to Albert that we must be leaving, that this is no place for Avi. But Albert he is telling me he can change this. He is saying to me that he was a soldier, a good German soldier, and that he must be talking to those people. Even the Nazis will remember that he fought so hard for Germany, he tells me. Those who fought in the First War, even if you are Jewish, you are left alone, there is no trouble for them. He is saying to me that they are treated as special men. He is also telling me that he is helping those people who cannot be paying the Nazi fines, helping them to be hiding or to be running to Hammelburg, where others are helping send them to Palestine or America."

She paused for a moment. "And I am saying back to him, people are screaming at you on the street, screaming at your son, a boy and no more. We must be going, I am saying to him. I am helping these people, he is saying. If I go, these people will not be getting to Hammelburg. Helping them I am because I am known, *Der Hebraisch Held,* a soldier from the First War. Such a man is this."

"That will be enough for now, I think," Belinda said.

On the morning following Sarah's death, I woke up alone in our bedroom, frightened and dazed. The confluence of anguish and disbelief, fear and incomprehensible listlessness, was grotesquely unique. I can fight this off, I thought, or I can just let it take me. The only thing that kept me from lying down and dying that day was that Sarah had to be properly memorialized and appropriately buried.

"*Verpflagen,*" Mrs. Silver said. "Be boarding. Get on to the boat," she called out to the memory of her husband. "*Verpflagen,*" she called again in a barely audible whisper. "*Verpflagen.*"

"Go and I will find you in Palestine," she repeated her husband's words. "I will be finding you. I must be staying. Without me there will be many more killings. I must be staying. Take Avi and go. I will find you.

"*Verpflagen,* Albert, please, please." She raised her hand and seemed to wave to his memory.

"Please, that will be enough for today," Belinda said.

"I want you to rest now. Please, I'm taking you to your room."

"Mrs. Schem?" Hannah said. "You are a very brave woman."

"There is not so much happiness in being brave."

I thought of all the questions Sarah would have wanted to ask. How had she survived all these years? What happened to Albert?

"Buchenwald," she replied, before Hannah could continue. "Albert is one of the first to be dying in Buchanwald. By the gun, they are shooting him for helping another with his work. For this he is killed. There was no chance to find us." As she finished speaking, Belinda turned the corner and they were gone.

For the next several minutes no one spoke or even moved.

"Are we done here, Sam?" Harry finally said.

Hersh pulled himself up and made his way to Hannah Cohen, and kissed her gently on the forehead. "A good start, I think."

Hannah blushed. "A good start."

MARCH 1948

"Are you a peddler?" a voice called. "We don't buy from street peddlers. If you need to see the rebbe, he's not here. Come back later."

"It's Elie Wasserman. I came to speak with Dina for a moment, if I could."

David Kishenev opened the door, glancing suspiciously at Elie. "You're the boy who hit Dina with the ball. I remember you."

Elie nodded.

"Why are you here?"

"I was hoping to speak with Dina for a moment. If she's home."

David's eyes were clearly his father's, large and light brown, and his demeanor was like Mrs. Kishenev, trusting and kind, yet unsure. He pulled on his long earlocks. "Well, since you're not a peddler, I suppose it's all right. Dina is with my mother. They should've been back already. When you knocked I thought — well —"

The door opened further, and Elie followed Dina's brother into the kitchen. Several books were open on the table. "I'm studying the Hadashim," he announced.

"The Hadashim is difficult, I don't know it well at all."

David's shoulders fell. "I actually wasn't reading the Hadashim. I was reading about the Warsaw Ghetto and the concentration camps." He pushed *The Black Book* toward Elie. Underneath was the description: *Essays and Illustrations of Crime known as The Final Solution.* "I'm supposed to be studying, but I'm not. I'm trying to figure out why people hate us."

Elie leafed through pages of photographs of victims lying in mass graves, clothes and eyeglasses in towering piles, and people huddled against barbed-wire fences, emaciated and lost. These were pictures he knew too well. His jaw tightened with anger.

"Please don't tell my parents I have this book in the house. They don't want Judah or Reyna to see these things. If my father knew it was here, he would be very angry. Are you going to tell them?"

"No, I promise."

"My father is afraid for me to see such things. And I heard him tell my mother that the twins shouldn't be exposed to such hatred. But, I'm twelve. I don't think that's too young."

"The pictures — they take away my breath," Elie said. "I think your father is right. The twins are too young."

"Have you seen them before?"

"Yes." Elie, too, had wondered about the origin of such hatred. He had spent hours in the library, staring at photographs of atrocities, trying to understand what drove people to such madness.

"My father says that the way to prevent this from happening again is to bring all the congregations together. To make us speak with one voice, he says. He says it's destructive to argue with each other over ritual. That's why Dina and Bernard will get married. That is why Dina . . . well . . ." He looked troubled.

From another room a clock chimed the hour.

"My mother isn't so happy about the engagement. It's just that Dina is always going on and on about love and silly things like that. My mother thinks Dina needs a lot of attention and she worries that Bernard won't be able to give it to her." He squinted at Elie. "Are you in love with my sister? I should probably not ask, but are you?"

"I just wanted to show her a letter I received. I thought she might be able to help me."

They heard the front door open. David hid the book on the Holocaust.

"David?" Mrs. Kishenev called.

"Yes, Mama."

Elie felt the chill from the open door and pulled his coat around him.

"Elie?" Dina whispered as she came into the kitchen. "I'm fine, Elie. Look. My bruises are almost gone. You should go and not worry about me any longer." She eyed her mother nervously. "Elie, you should go. Father does not think you should be here, and he'll be home soon." She tried to look stern.

"Your father welcomes everyone in our home," Mrs. Kishenev said. "Don't say such things."

"I just needed to show you this letter." He reached into his pocket.

Elie saw Mrs. Kishenev and Dina's eyes meet.

"I'm not here to interfere, I promise." He waited for a response, but Mrs. Kishenev seemed satisfied. "This is a letter from someone who may have known my father. Well, at least he can tell me some things about my past. It's a start. Rabbi Kishenev was right. I should know more about these things and my mother should have this resolved. She gave me the name of this man from Freiburg. He's said he'll talk to me — well, his sister said he'd talk to me — and my mother wants me to do this." Elie handed the letter to Mrs. Kishenev. "I need Dina's help for a very short time if it's all right with you and with the rebbe."

Mrs. Kishenev read the letter aloud.

Dear Elie,

I have received your letter you have written to my brother Menachem. As you now know from your mother, my brother did know your father some. They both were raised in Freiburg and my brother speaks very well of him.

Unfortunately, my brother is no longer well. His seeing is bad and is very poor and he has many serious problems with his legs. He must sit all the time now as his legs are very weak. Also, due to his illnesses he cannot leave the house and he has had very few visitors over the last years.

In spite of this, after I received your letter I asked if he would be able to tell you anything of your father and of Freiburg. He said that he was able to do this and that if you did not stay long, he would try to help you.

I have told him you would be here on Tuesday evening next as you asked. You said that was a day when you were not at work in the store or at school. I hope this is still when you will come. I am there only on Thursdays. I hope this will not keep you from coming.

Please, however, I must make one request before your visit. If it is possible, I would ask that you did not come alone. Menachem is a nice man, but he is also full of fear. Perhaps your mother would be able to join you. I know her and she is a nice woman.

I have told him to expect you on Tuesday. Still he may not remember. Knock on the door and wait. He will come.

Sincerely, Elke Kultz

"Why do you need my help?" Dina asked. "I can't go with you. I'm far too busy."

Dina waited for her mother to agree, but Mrs. Kishenev did not speak. "I must work tonight. I have to clean all the silver and sweep and mop. Then I have to dust and take the fingermarks off the crystal." She gave the letter back to Elie. "I have reading to do also, and then . . . and then I must write a letter to Bernard . . . So I can't go with you."

"What has your mother told you of this man?" Mrs. Kishenev asked.

"He and my father knew each other during the First War. And that he could tell me things about Freiburg. She told me that Mr. Kultz knows stories of my father's days during the war. And that he knows some of what happened after the war before we left Freiburg. How my father helped people."

"Have you contacted the service yet or Frana Luftwantz?"

"I've written them a letter. I sent it to Frana Luftwantz as the rabbi instructed. I haven't heard anything yet, though." Elie replaced Elke Kultz's letter in his pocket. "Please tell the rabbi that he was very helpful last week and that I appreciate his advice. And that my mother does also."

"Who will go with you?" Dina asked.

"Yudie, I suppose. He'll tell me not to bother, but I'll tell him it's important. He'll come."

Dina turned to face him. "You'd take Yudie Kosasky on a visit such as this? Yudie Kosasky who knows only how to insult and make those around him worry for the next words that come from his mouth. He's a tyrant. He won't listen. He'll only speak as he always does, like someone with a sewing pin in his shoe. And he'll certainly frighten this poor man. I've never been with him when he didn't wear the face of a pirate or an oppressor. He reminds me of all things that are unpleasant. I know he's your friend," she said more gently, "but if this man is fearful, Yudie will scare the stories from his memory altogether. You should take someone else."

"Dina, get your coat and go with Elie," Mrs. Kishenev said. "It'll be all right."

"But Papa will be angry with me."

"For helping a family who has asked for your aid? I don't think so."

"Bernard will be angry then. He'll think of this as betrayal. He'll never forgive me."

"I promise you, my daughter, Bernard Liebenshul will not lift his nose from the Kodashim long enough to know that you have been gone for a short time. Even you know him better than that. Go now. Give Elie your help." Mrs. Kishenev exhaled and relaxed. "Where does this man live, Elie?"

"In the Square, above Levin's. We won't stay long, I promise. I just want him to be comfortable."

"Mama? Mama, I . . . "

"Go now. It's all right, Dina. It's the right thing to do. Watch over my daughter, Elie Wasserman."

They walked for many blocks in silence. When Elie noticed that she was trembling, he gave Dina his gloves.

"Elie, you can't keep coming to the house," Dina said at last. She stopped on the sidewalk and grabbed Elie by the sleeve. "I . . . I'm going to be married. I have to be with Bernard Liebenshul. I'm not so selfish as to think that I am more important than the community. He needs my help. He needs me. He needs me to show everyone that he understands more than just books and treatises."

"When I received the letter from Elke Kultz," Elie said, "I thought of you, that's all. I could've asked Yudie. I guess I should have. You're right, though, Yudie makes people nervous. I need to listen to what Mr. Kultz has to say. I don't get many chances to hear about Freiburg or why we left or about my father. I didn't mean to make it difficult for you."

"I can't. I . . . I can't be with you. It's too late. We can't . . . You don't understand. You just can't keep coming by and being so nice to everyone. First it was Judah and Reyna, now David. I have to be ready to help Bernard. I'm afraid of not being there when he needs me. This is part of me. It's what I am and what I have to be."

She began to cry. "When I came to see you the other night in the back of the store," she whispered, "I think that was — I wished that I could have stayed there with you, our bodies tangled together forever. Every time we're together, I think that. I thought later, laying in my bed at home: Wouldn't it have been nice if we could have fallen asleep there like Rip Van Winkle? Sleeping, huddled together, in that storeroom for twenty years. For one hundred years. I wanted that feeling to last forever. I'm afraid I won't ever feel like that again. I don't think I will."

"Your father wouldn't want that, you know. He wouldn't want to know how sad you are. He would —"

Dina gripped his arm. "You must never say anything. Right here, you must promise never to speak to my father about this."

"I promise. I promise." He turned to her and kissed her forehead. "What's he like?"

"What do you mean?"

"Bernard, what's he like? What do you know about him?"

"He's very nice."

"All I know about him is that he's supposed to be a genius and the next rebbe of the Khal Anshei Chessed. And that your father thinks he is the Messiah, according to David."

"He tells jokes sometimes. He's very funny."

"The new rebbe of the Khal Anshei Chessed tells jokes?"

"He does. I'll tell you one that he told me." Dina struggled. "I can't remember any."

"This horse is having a bad day," Elie said "So he goes into shul to see the rabbi. The rabbi looks at him and says: 'So what's with the long face?' "

Dina giggled. They walked again and their hands came together.

A grim wind blew by as they reached the hallway leading to the apartment. The steep stairs were dim and shabby. Together, they read the mailbox, looking for Menachem Kultz. "I'm glad you came with me," Elie said, looking up the stairs. "And I'm sorry if I teased you about Bernard. I won't —"

"The other night I overheard my mother tell my father that you're confusing me," she interrupted him. "About Bernard. They're nervous when you come by. They know you confuse me."

"I'm not trying to confuse you. Honestly. I'm not. I just — It just seems like for as long as I can remember I have had this feeling. That I'm waiting. Waiting for something to happen or for somebody to . . ." He tried to think of the right words. "I've always waited for my father to come home; to walk through the door and save my mother. I waited for my mother to tell me where I came from and how we got here to Mattapan, but she always told me to wait for my father; that he could tell me all those things. I waited for somebody — my mother, a teacher, somebody — to tell me I could be a journalist like my father — a good journalist — and that I didn't have to work like my mother or be a hardware salesman. I waited for the priests to change their minds and give me the prize I won." He smiled, then grew solemn. "I remember, even as a little kid, waiting in long lines to board trains or boats. Waiting for food. Waiting with strangers. It just seems like I've always been waiting. I don't guess that I know you very well, but when I'm with you, I don't feel like I am waiting anymore."

"I . . . I don't think I can see you again after tonight," Dina said. "I have to marry Bernard. I need to be ready for my responsibilities. I can't disappoint my father, I can't."

They each waited for the other to speak. "I won't ask you again. I promise," Elie finally said. "I believe in your father also."

They the stairs together. Dina took Elie's hand again. There was no sound, only their footsteps.

A window at the far end of the corridor let in just enough light from the Square to allow them to see their way.

Elie knocked softly. There was a cough, then silence. Again Elie knocked.

"Elke? My Elke, is that you?"

"Mr. Kultz, it's Elie Wasserman. I wrote to you. Your sister told us we might be able to speak with you. My mother is Lena Wasserman. We came from Freiburg. You knew my father. You knew him in Freiburg."

There was no response. "Your sister said I should not come alone, Mr. Kultz."

"And who is with you?" Menachem Kultz asked. He was closer to the door. "One of the hoodlums from the street? You'd like to take some of my things perhaps? Or have you come to clop me on the head?"

"I came with Elie. My name is Dina Kishenev."

The latch turned and the door inched open. A face peered out, and inspected them. "It's all right. Come in, my young ones. Come in. Come in."

"I'm Dina —"

"Ah, my child, I know who you are. Before I was so weak I would sit in the park and watch the children. Elke would tell me: There is the Rebbe Kishenev's beautiful daughter. Such a child that is, she would say. And so nice with her brothers and sisters and the other children."

To Elie, Menachem Kultz appeared old. His hair was gone, except for the few loose strands of white over his ears. His skin was pale and thin and his clothes were frayed with age. He was confined to a wheelchair.

"I don't look well for my age," he said to Elie, "but this does not mean I'm angry. People worry that with a face like this, I will treat them as if I am an old kvetcher or a *shmata*. This is before they even talk to me. Eh, sometimes even after they talk to me. I'll make a promise to you. I'm not an unpleasant man."

Elie wanted to say that he had made no such assumption, but he had and he was sorry.

"I am glad to be here," Dina said.

"Tea, my guests? You will have beautiful children, you two. You are both so handsome. Please, if you are here for conversation, you must both call me Menachem."

They glanced at each other in tacit agreement not to speak of Dina's betrothal to Bernard Liebenshul. Nevertheless, Elie explained to Mr. Kultz that they were just friends.

"Do you pray at Khal Anshei Chessed?" asked Dina.

"Here in my house is where I pray, my dear." He pointed to a shelf filled with prayer books, *tefilin,* and Yiddish literature. "For young people to follow their hearts, that is what I pray for." He closed his eyes mumbled in Yiddish. "There, I've asked God for help in that regard. Now, how about some warm tea?"

Mr. Kultz pushed himself toward the small hotplate on the table by the window. Nearby, were a sugar bowl, cups, and saucers. The kettle rested on the windowsill, out of reach, but Mr. Kultz poked at it with a cane. "My Elke, she puts everything just in its place, so I can reach it. She set out these cups for us." He moved the teakettle onto the stove.

"Your mother has not come in quite some time," he informed Elie. "My memory of such things is not so good, but I think it has been many years. I remember, she said that someday she would send you here. When she was ready. She is well?"

"Fine."

"Sit down, my young friends. I'm glad you have come. It is not often that I get to speak of the past to those who were not present for the events."

"I wish my mother had told me about you sooner. My father's past, I only know it in bits and pieces. My mother is afraid to speak about him because it is admitting that he'll never come to Mattapan."

"Don't be too hard on your mother. Her life hasn't been an easy one. Sometimes people hold on to hope as if it was their own skin. Without it, they feel they would just fall into pieces."

Elie wondered what hope Mr. Kultz could have. None, he supposed, but the man seemed without bitterness.

"My friends, could you bring out the trunk from under my bed? The black one, if you don't mind. Bring it to us here."

Elie did as he was asked and returned to his seat, and Mr. Kultz handed each of his guests a cup of tea.

"My mother says that you knew my father," Elie said, taking a sip. "Did you know him well?'

"Did you work at the Aben . . . the *Abenpost* also?" Dina asked.

"No. No. At the Werkzeugmaschine die Fabrik. I was nothing more than a *mahkh-shee-rim-mah-khehr,* a toolmaker. An apprentice. Moving papers and boxes from here to there and back."

"So how did you know him?" Elie asked.

"We were together, in the First Army, your father and I. That is where I came to know him . . . in the Freiburg *Bekampfen.*"

"We have a picture in our flat." Elie nodded. "He's in his uniform. I didn't know what outfit he was with. I know he fought bravely."

"So many were in the First. Such proud soldiers we were." He grimaced. "God was with us, so we thought. He had to be."

"What do you mean?" Dina said.

"We believed we had a noble mission. Everyone was behind us. Everywhere, the words were written: To Brussels, To Paris, To London. On the walls. On the buildings. On the streetcars. There was cheering and crying for joy. People ran out from the sidewalks and gave to us as we passed. Chocolates or sweaters or even money. Like heroes we were, and we had not yet seen even one enemy soldier. Nothing could stop us. We had been told again and again that war, for young men, this was exciting. Fighting for your country, this was noble. Dying, this couldn't happen if the cause was good. We could not be defeated."

Elie and Dina were riveted.

"We were to march through Belgium, and then to the west and keep the French from the sea. Then, of course, we would circle Paris and together with other armies storm the capital, and end the war in a week's time. What could be wrong? God, he was watching over us and we would be marching home with victory."

Mr. Kultz leaned down and whispered something to Dina that made her laugh. Elie loved her smile. He thought of her father, then, and wondered whether the rebbe ever worried that the marriage might not work to draw the congregations together as he had planned. Did he know, Elie asked himself, how devoted Dina was? Did he truly believe that Dina loved Bernard, as she bravely maintained? Her mother did not seem convinced.

Mr. Kultz opened the latch, pulled a gray tunic from the trunk, and spread it over his knees. There were shreds in the sleeves at the shoulders and the cloth was stained. The stripes of rank were sewn onto the collar and also into the sleeves at the shoulder. "*Der Lansers,* that is what I was. This, your father was also."

Elie recognized the stripes from the picture of his father. "Our photograph is faded. But that's the same uniform."

"We were not ready for how frightened we were to become. They didn't tell us how many would die and for how long we would have to crouch down in the cold. We did not hear the French had developed artillery and shells twice again as large as had ever been fired before. Or that the English, with their training in Africa, had guns that could shoot out our eyes at a mile's distance." Elie watched him shudder. "No one told us the Belgian King would cut open his own dikes in the Polders and drown thousands of German soldiers, as well as his own. And, we weren't warned that French mutineers were roaming the country, killing as they went, as if insanity had overtaken them all."

"Being brave is not so easy," Dina said.

"Even with these terrors, there was no man who respected his obligation to his country more than your father. Not once in the cold did he complain, even while the rest of us whined that our fingers were stiff. If there was not enough food, to the younger soldiers he would give them his bread. A volunteer you need; your father was the first to step forward. Always it was like this. This is why when you left with your mother, he stayed. That is why he stayed, despite your mother begging him. To show Hitler the Jews should not be blamed."

Elie wondered whether he had his father's strength of character and determination. "My mother told me that she wished more than anything that it would've been enough for my father to have saved us that night; that he would have understood then what was coming and come with us. I guess he wasn't selfish enough. Otherwise, he would be here."

"He thought he could save others," Dina said. "He wasn't selfish at all."

"I guess not," Elie said.

"Many men thanked your father for their lives during the First War," Kultz said. "I myself. I owe my life to him. Always those around him he thought of, then himself. That you and your mother were saved because someone remembered his bravery from the First War could only have meant to your father that his obligation was to stay. Always the others first, not himself."

"Mr. Wasserman saved your life?" Dina asked.

"How many he saved at Passchendaele," he whispered, "only God himself knows this."

Mr. Kultz mumbled a prayer to himself. Dina rose and kneeled at the foot of his wheelchair. She took his hands in hers. "You are a brave and strong man. And I'm so proud to have met you. I am going to tell my father all about you, about Emil Wasserman also. He'll write sermons about such bravery. And tell these stories to all the congregations, Ohub Zedek, Congregation Sfath Emes. Perhaps Elie will write about these events someday."

"All for a country that would call us monsters."

"Are you okay?" Dina said. "If it's too difficult —"

He patted her hand. "The fighting you see, it went on without stopping. Your father and I, we performed the Teshuvah on Rosh Hashanah and we fasted on Yom Kippur, there in our trench. On the Sabbath we drank dirty water and said the prayer over the wine even though we had none. God's minyan we called ourselves. We were not ten, but we thought God would permit us this one small transgression." He nodded to himself.

"In the fall — 1916 this was — the First, we held the ground to the east of Passchendaele. There were other armies there also. We dug holes into the ground to protect ourselves. Trenches."

Elie pictured his father sitting with his gun between his knees and his back to the inside of a trench. His helmet was on and he was waiting, silently, for the chaos that would follow.

"When the rains came, just before spring, so did the shelling. Our lines at Ypres and at Messines Ridge were shelled first. Even from the distance, the sound of shelling shakes your heart, your insides. The French 75. The noise is everywhere, and so loud the ears go cold with ringing. And where they land, it blows a wind that is hot, like fire — fire filled with the smell of flesh. A terrible smell. From Passchendaele we sat with our heads down and listened to other men die and smelled their dying."

Elie saw Dina shift uneasily.

"And then the rain came. Oye, such rain. Down and down. Day after day. Like the sky had opened and God poured water on us to keep us awake and cold. And still shells falling out of the sky, closer and closer to us and so loud. A shell would fall and with it a man's blood. Nothing more. What happened to the rest?" He rubbed his legs as if to reassure himself they were still there. "Your father and I, we held each other and prayed to God to help us. All around us, everywhere, explosions. So close, with each one we thought our lives had ended."

He tried to sip his tea but the cup trembled in his hand and he replaced it on the saucer. "The sky was black above us even in the day. We were not certain if this was from the rain or from the smoke from the shells. So dark it was, the only light was from the explosions. It lasted for days without stopping. For days. And for the nights as well.

"And then — and then, it stopped. For an hour we waited, and then another hour. Too afraid we were to put our heads up. But then we did. Men could not imagine such a thing as we saw there. The world was destroyed — burned. As far as could be seen, there was nothing. Only mud and holes where shells had fallen. Trees stood now crooked and with the branches gone; all of them, just broken sticks rising from the mud. This patch of earth was to fight for? God should open up the heavens and take this patch. This was land that belonged only to the dead."

He ran his hand along the sleeve of the uniform laying on his lap. "Only then did we hear from our captains: The enemy was coming. Many thousands had died to the west of us in fighting. We had to move. 'Hurry,' they said, 'save whatever artillery you can. But go quickly.' " Elie could see his disgust at this order. "Where ten men on dry land could move this artillery, now fifty men with ropes could not pull the guns from the mud. Where the shells had left holes, if a gun rolled from the ridge, underneath the mud it would go and be swallowed up entirely. Men, they saw this, and they wept. The enemy would simply overrun us and we would die, we thought. There was little that could be done."

A soft rain tapped against the window and he paused to listen.

"Finally the word came. 'Get off the lowlands. Pull back. Leave everything.' After all this bombing. After so many had already died.

"There were five of us that I remember. Besides your father and myself, there was Frederick Unger, a boy. Johan Plotz, he was shoemaker with seven children at home. And Schmitt. Karl Schmitt. He talked only of his wife. Nothing else ever came from his mouth. All from Freiburg, that is why I remember."

Elie wanted to ask his mother if she knew these names.

"Schmitt and Plotz, it was their turn to be looking for the signal to move. The rain was coming down very hard. So difficult to see, it was. But, in the distance, in the darkness they saw the lantern. We all looked. We agreed. Yes."

To Elie he appeared to be searching again, in his imagination, for the signal.

"Then, as we crawled, the shelling again."

"Why did they . . . How?" Dina began, but couldn't finish.

"A shell came near to us, that's all I remember. An explosion. So loud, it was like a hammer had come down on my ear. And then — I'm in a hole. And there is screaming close by to me. Some of the others are in this hole too. This hole, there is water in it, but I can feel it is mostly mud. Beneath the water is mud. And I'm sinking."

Elie's heart pounded.

"Another shell went off and in its light, I saw Frederick Unger near me. A terrible look on his face. I reached for him. I stretched my arm. But then the next light came, and only his hand was above the mud. From the light of one shell to the next, he went below the mud."

Elie thought Dina might cry.

"Your father and Plotz, 'Call out,' they shouted at us. 'Call out, we can't see you. Call out. Sing something,' they said. 'Sing and keep singing. Sing *Deutschland uber Alles.*' And there Schmitt and I, sinking in the mud, we are singing like fools."

He shuddered again. "I remember thinking, the French, they will hear us, that somewhere below the mud, Unger could hear us also. I wondered if he died with this song in his ears."

Elie watched as Kultz relived the night he described, his face contorted in pain.

"Schmitt, he begged Plotz to shoot him when light let them see."

"Oh, God," Dina said. "No." She covered her mouth with both hands.

"'Sing,' your father screamed at him."

Elie caressed Dina's arm. "Wait," he said to her.

"We could all see with the next shell that only his face was above the mud. Just his face."

Elie felt a chill as he imagined Schmitt fighting to remain above the mire.

"Schmitt, he went under the mud. Once the mud held you by the legs — well the legs, they could not move then. It was like tar. 'Stay above the mud,' I shouted at him. *Baruch ata adonois, elohanuh melech ha-o-lum,* over and over. To my neck, and then to my ears. *Baruch ata adonois elohanuh melech ha-o-lum.*" He gripped the handles of his chair, and choked back words. "Then, I was below the mud."

Elie felt a lump in his throat. For an instant he was below the mud, alone, dying.

"I felt my chest grow tight. I thought it was my heart stopping; that this was suffocating; your lungs being gripped like a vice. I began to struggle and to shake and to fight." Elie watched Kultz's eyes fill with tears and his hands begin to shudder again.

"But it was not my heart. My lungs were not collapsing."

Elie took Dina's hand and squeezed it. Kultz fell back into his chair and paused to let the trembling stop.

"Your father's arms were around me. His strength was inconceivable to me. He would not let go no matter how the mud pulled me back; he wouldn't let go; he didn't let go." He wiped his eyes. "He was tied to he others. They pulled us back. I was dead — and then I wasn't."

Elie was brimming with pride and excitement. Dina kissed his hand.

"Schmitt too. He saved us both. He had nearly killed himself to save us. Mud came from his mouth and he coughed and spit dirt. Schmitt, he just coughed and prayed."

Elie imagined the four men caked with mud, lying on the bank of wet earth, each thanking God that they were alive.

"My collarbone was broken. But, whatever pain there was, I was glad for. I was still breathing."

"My father must hear this," Dina said.

"My mother should not have waited so long," Elie murmured.

"Everyone who goes to war has stories. Sometimes they seem more important than they are."

"Are there others still alive who knew my father?"

"I don't know. If the war had ended differently, your father would have been known to everyone. Schmitt, I know, told everyone about this man who swam beneath the mud. *Der Hebraisch Held,* he called him. *Der Hebraish Held. Der Hebraish Held.* He told everyone."

"The Hebrew Hero," Elie said to Dina, reminding her of their earlier conversation with her mother and father.

She nodded.

"My mother mentioned that people called him that. I'm so glad to know why." He felt proud and full of energy. "Can you tell me more?"

They walked down Blue Hill Avenue, passed Simco's on the Bridge, and turned onto Fessenden Street. Near a flickering gas lamp, Elie glanced at Dina. He did not want this walk home to end.

"I'm sorry it is so late," he apologized. "Your mother's going to be angry with me. Are you okay?" Dina bit her lip. "You're not usually so quiet. I didn't know —"

At the steps leading to the shul, Dina stopped and took his hand in hers. "I'm glad you asked me to go with you. It seemed like we met your father tonight. I felt sometimes like I was there in the trench with him." She dropped his hand and walked toward the door to the house. Elie watched her for a moment and then followed at a run. He caught her by the elbow as she turned into the doorway.

"Papa?" Elie heard her say. He looked up at the entrance to the foyer. Rebbe Kishenev was there.

"Papa? Papa?" The rebbe was ashen and somber. He

had been crying. Elie wondered whether he had been searching for Dina, and his heart, too, began to pound.

"Elie Wasserman," the rebbe said. "Another injury? I hope not."

"Papa, what happened? Tell me what has happened."

"God in his wisdom, has taken Rebecah Moffensohn tonight. A child of six, He has taken tonight. A beautiful child — so beautiful she was. Pale and beautiful."

"Oh, Papa."

"I told Mrs. Moffensohn that God has a reason for everything. That God has infinite wisdom and that he always does what's best. Mrs. Moffensohn, she asked why God would take a child. How such a thing could be explained as God knowing always what was right and what was good.

"I told her the truth. That there was no explanation nor any good reason — even for God — to take Rebecah. God had made a mistake. Would it have been so terrible to make everything all right instead? Come into the house now, Dina. Elie, it is time for you to go home." He stepped inside the foyer and left them alone

Elie stepped toward Dina and kissed her forehead. "Thank you for coming with me. Tell your father I'm sorry. That must have been very difficult for him."

He was several steps away, when he felt her behind him. He turned and their bodies came together and their lips met.

"I love you," Dina said. "I love you. I love you." Her eyes held his longingly. "Please be happy for me. I miss you already."

Elie watched as she ran into the house.

JULY 1991

I mulled the fate of Albert Schem through most of the late afternoon and during that evening's meal as well. The story confused me, but not because the facts were unclear. Rather, it was because my reaction to it swung so widely between extremes. I would, one moment, be lamenting his demise; couching his torturous death in terms of heroic loyalty — somewhat akin to the brave rabbi in Russia described earlier, I thought. The next moment I would be reviling him as the enemy; a despicable man who had probably killed dozens of Americans in World War I (men, I was also convinced, who had fought alongside and protected my own father during those harrowing times). "*Chazzer,*" I would repeat under my breath, when I considered his misbegotten patriotism. But how, I would immediately think, can I condemn one of my own — a member of the community of Jews — no matter how unsavory I considered his history.

That night, in my room, my frustration intensified. I told myself that his beleaguered destiny was simply none of my concern fifty years after his death. "What difference does it make," I said aloud. But when I tried to read I could not erase the image of Albert Schem — a faceless soldier — dug into a trench, his Kaiser Cross intertwined with the *mezuzah* around his neck, as he aimed round after round at the brave Allies across the field.

I fell asleep muttering to myself, trying to understand what he could have been thinking when he refused to leave Freiburg that grim gray day in 1938.

The next morning on the porch, I closed my eyes and pretended to be asleep, almost as if I were hiding. With my head back and my book overturned in my lap, I listened, as Hersh and Hannah began a curious discussion.

"When I came here, I was so nervous," Hannah whispered. "I didn't want to be a burden on anyone, the nurses or anyone. I just thought I'd keep to myself; not bother anyone, do my reading. I didn't want to be in anyone's way. You've changed all that. When I'm here, on the porch with you, it seems different. I'm different. I want to try to do things I didn't think were possible before. That to be honest I never thought of . . . I . . ."

"You're the inspiration for this enterprise," Hersh said.

I had the impression they were holding hands or he was caressing her face.

"You're a wonderful man. I didn't think I could fall in love again, but I may be in love with you. Is it too soon for me to tell you this?"

"And with you it's impossible for me not to have such feelings."

"I'm not so lovable in this chair, looking like I do."

"You're beautiful," he said. "Why would you think such a thing? My breath is taken away when we are together. I'm so lucky to have found you. Every minute I count my blessings. Every single minute."

They did not speak for a while. It was a rare gift to be able to drift away into silence while in such close proximity to someone and not grow uncomfortable with the quiet. Such ease, I thought, is the exclusive province of spouses — of the happily married variety at that — or perhaps, on rare occasions, of best friends.

What about their marriages; had they been happy? Fulfilling? Were there warm memories? Since Sarah died I had no companionship at all. I pictured myself as a toothless vagabond, huddled behind my books, engaged in odd voyeurism, invading the privacy of others for my sole source of entertainment. Nauseating!

"Would it be so terrible just to write a short story," I heard Maury Margolis in the background. He was somewhere near the door. "Would it be so terrible? We're just a bunch of *alte cockers.*"

I thought back to my own attempt at writing fiction forty years earlier, and about how difficult it had been for me to concentrate on work that was so easy to put aside. Sarah encouraged me, bringing me coffee at all hours, never letting on she knew I wasn't ready to write, that my commitment was just not there.

"We just have to concentrate," Hannah assured him. "All of us."

I had not simply quit. There had been no announcement from me that I could not do it. Instead, I began to use any excuse I could concoct not to sit at the typewriter; anything at all so long as I was able to convince myself it was legitimate. Then one day, the dream was so far behind me that I couldn't go back. Sarah had never said one word about my failure.

"It would have been nice to have actually tried," I said aloud.

"I'm sorry, Abe, I . . . didn't hear you," Hannah Cohen said, her words trailing off.

The following day, at least until the mail arrived, Hersh and Hannah conferred at their table, their affinity for one another's company evidenced by the proximity of their chairs that seemed to inch closer together as the minutes passed. This drawing nearer seemed almost magnetic, as if it occurred by the force of their wills, rather than by any physical efforts. Regardless, they were soon nearly collapsed upon each other; close enough, in any event, to touch, which they did with increasing frequency.

I watched them, surreptitiously over the edge of my book.

"What if we put them all together," she suggested, "the Albert Schem story, Rose's story, and pieces of some of the others." I raised my eyes to look at them.

"The stories can be put together?" Hersh asked.

Hannah gazed at Hersh with an expression of earnestness and sincerity. "I think so — I think so." She was immersed in her thoughts and silent for nearly a minute. "During, no after, the Second World War. A love story," she said. "The two main characters can meet during a basketball game — like in Mel's story."

I glanced around the room but no one else was listening. "The boy will be playing and take the last shot to win the game, but he will miss and hit the girl in the forehead. She will be reading and not be paying any attention as she walks by, like my friend Bea. That's how they meet."

"So far I'm with you," Hersh said.

"Wait, let me — She'll be the daughter of a rabbi. And she'll be promised to another rabbi's son. Do you think we could use the name Dina? I always loved that name."

"Any name you want is what we'll use."

She closed her eyes and massaged her temples, then tapped one finger on the table. "She'll be promised to the other rabbi's son because her father wants to merge the two congregations together, and he thinks it's the only way. Because they're afraid. Like Rose's story. Afraid of another Holocaust. After he hits her with the ball, they'll talk and then fall in love. And the boy," she said with rising excitement, "he'll be the son of Albert Schem. He'll live with his mother; his father will have been a German soldier in the First War who remained behind because he thought he could help the other Jews. He was remembered and respected for his efforts during the First War. But now we'll say he is lost, not dead. Everyone will think he is dead. Assume it. But they won't know for sure."

Hersh's excitement matched hers.

"This boy, he'll help Dina home after he hits her — Yes. And the rabbi, her father, will convince him that he has to look for his father. That he must find out what happened to him. We can make it that he doesn't know because his mother's made him promise not to investigate. She's too frightened about what he'll find. But the rabbi will tell him that he must help his mother go on with her life. That if he doesn't, she'll be nothing more than another casualty of the Holocaust." She clearly liked her story. "Yes. And in the process of trying to help him find his father, Dina and this boy will fall in love, even though she's promised to the other boy."

"Good," Hersh prodded her. "What happens?"

"If it would be okay, I was hoping that — that it could all work out. I know I'm a bit old-fashioned. Would it be so terrible to have a happy ending?"

"Happiness is my best thing."

"With Dina's help, he can find out his father is alive, but lost after a long stay in a concentration camp. He was very strong, remember. He was a war hero." She glanced at Hersh hopefully. "And then the boy can go back to the rabbi and tell him that Dina shouldn't be another victim of the Holocaust. That they can't let fear force them to make choices. And the rabbi will realize his mistake and let them be together, Dina and this boy.

"It needs to be fleshed out some, I know." She was

worried, I sensed, that she had not fully explained her plot. "But I can feel this. This story — we're fated to write it. That's why we're here. Together. You and me."

It would have been nice for Sarah to know Hannah, I thought. I imagined them chatting over coffee; they would have been the dearest of friends. Good God, I screamed in my mind, forcing the thought to disappear.

The reason for my anger was that I was envious. I wanted, once again , to feel as if I could put words to paper, to be memorialized in black and white, to be published! I was haunted as a young man by the notion that in every man there is one great novel. I had tried mysteries, morality plays, and Dickensian tales of childhood woes; I attempted romances, adventures, children's books. Nothing came of it but failure.

"It can have a wonderful ending, full of hope and optimism," Hannah Cohen said. "I hope people cry from happiness at the end."

I shook off my reverie and watched as Hersh touched Hannah Cohen's fingers, then caressed her cheek. This hand holding and ogling on the porch is embarrassing, I lectured them silently. Enough already. "Listen —" But my mouth was too dry and the word came out as gravel.

"Are you okay, Abe?" Belinda shouted. "Abe?"

I coughed to clear my throat. "Yes, I'm fine."

"I think we should get started right away," Hersh declared.

"Belinda, do you have a pen or a pencil, dear?" Hannah said. She turned to Hersh. "Would you mind if I wrote down some thoughts as we discuss this?"

I was thunderstruck. They might actually see the project through. It was no longer a question of when they would quit, but when they would finish. The actual writing would be full of pitfalls. But they had crossed some threshold, and now had the momentum to complete the project. I also understood they were in this alone; the others would fall away slowly, leaving just the two of them.

I felt a prickly heat rise through my neck and settle at the back of my head. Hersh smirked at me. "Why are you staring?" I asked.

MARCH 1948

The flat seemed quiet. The radio was off. Elie called to his mother.

"In the kitchen, I am." Her voice was weak. "Come, Come sit with me. I have tea."

Elie closed the door and hung up his coat, then joined his mother.

"I went to see the rebbe today," she told him. "I didn't go to work. I said that I was sick." She stared into her cup. "I called Isaac Zelton. I said that I was sick."

"Are you?"

"No."

"Why did you need to see Rebbe Schecter? It must have been important if you decided not to go to work."

"Not Rebbe Schecter. I went to see Rebbe Kishenev. I went to Adas Yeraim."

Elie's heart skipped. "What? Why?" He was embarrassed for a moment.

"I took over a kugel. I wanted to see her face. Mrs. Shetzel, she said it was the right thing to do."

"I hit her a long time ago. Her eye is fine now."

She shifted uneasily in her chair. "Mrs. Shetzel says that last night you were with her."

Elie pulled up a chair and sat. "She — that lady should

mind her own damn business. She makes me want to shake her."

"Shh. Don't talk like that. Anyway she's right. You shouldn't be interfering with these plans of hers, even though, yes, she's a wonderful girl. I told the mother we wouldn't interfere."

"I thought you went to see the rebbe?"

She shrugged. "He wasn't there, so I sat with the mother. What is so terrible? And yes, Dina, she came later also — and the other children. The small ones. They talk about you."

"I took her with me to see Mr. Kultz. That's where we went. Elke Kultz told me not to go alone. You can tell Mrs. Shetzel that."

His mother sipped her tea and peered at him over her cup, expressing her disappointment at his tone.

"She went on about your father, this Dina. A talker she is."

"They are stories people should know. I might want to write about them someday myself." Elie wondered about the families of the men who died in the mud before his father could reach them. "Papa was brave. And respected. These are important stories."

"Your father, he would not tell me such stories. Others told me. He did not speak of himself. This was not his way." She dabbed at some tea that had spilled on the saucer. "But there was never a kinder man."

She began to hum a lullaby and Elie could see the song brought her joy. "This he would sing to you, and rock you on his lap. Every night to sleep, just with your father. This, I suppose, you don't remember?"

"No. My earliest memory, my first memory is of an older man with a beard and a big face, a round face, but I know that wasn't him."

"No," she agreed. "No." She waited for Elie to continue.

"We were in a crowd of people somewhere and you were holding me by the shoulder against your leg. I remember him bending down to talk to me. That's all. I don't know where we were. It was crowded. I remember that."

"A train station somewhere. There were so many."

Their journey, Elie knew, had taken them first to Switzerland, where they were cared for, together with other refugees, by a Swiss relief organization, then to Croydon in England for several months, followed by boat to Montreal, and a bus to Chicago.

"I knew your father would send us away. I could see his worry. He knew from the paper that there was danger, and he knew of these plans this terrible man had for the Jews. He wrote about it in the *Abenpost*."

Elie felt dread spilling over him. "He should have followed us. He could have come."

"We were very lucky to get out. So many were not allowed to go. No one would take so many Jews. No one wanted us." She slumped on the sofa. "Thank God for Mordechi."

Mordechi Huddle was an uncle of Elie's father. He had been nearly eighty when Elie and his mother reached Chicago, but was most generous with his home. Elie remembered him for his kindness; his fingers were something Elie would never forget. They had become crooked and swollen from years of using scissors at the textile factory, and they appeared broken and useless. To Elie, they had felt like stones.

"Your father, he promised he would follow us to Mordechi's. He wrote this in his letters."

"Mordechi told me he wouldn't come," Elie confessed.

His mother didn't seem to hear. "You remember Mordechi? Into his apartment, big enough only for himself, he took us. He was kind to us. Poor Mordechi. May he rest in peace."

"I remember him. I remember his fingers. Just before he died. He told me Papa wasn't going to be allowed to travel here, and that I was going to have to grow up and take care of you. That was the first time I remember wondering whether we would ever see Papa again. You said we would. But from that day on, I had my doubts."

Her hands began to shake. "Perhaps in Chicago we should have stayed. Perhaps your father, he could have found us if we had stayed. I . . . I didn't know what to do. I . . . After Mordechi was gone, I wanted to give you a home, but I was uncertain. I was —"

"Please don't —"

"I was so lonely. I didn't know what was the right thing to do. And still my heart, it aches with loneliness. Every day this aching. Some days I feel like not another minute can I live this way. My head won't hold such pain. And now — now." Anxiety gripped her. "I don't want you to feel this loneliness. Ever. Please, I'm begging you. Do not wonder about her, this Dina. You cannot be with her. Do not think any more about her. No more. You are my son. I do not want you to feel this sadness I feel. Please. Please."

Elie thought of their kiss the night before. He longed for Dina. His mother's words were bewildering. He wanted to shout that the proposed marriage wasn't right.

"I'm thinking you are in love with this Dina and that she's in love with you. I see this in her. But Rebbe Kishenev and Rebbe Liebenshul have decided for her. Mrs. Kishenev has decided for her. I am worried, Elie."

Elie was momentarily terrified. What if letting them be married is the right thing to do, he thought. How many people bore the scars of loss? How many were left without fathers, without mothers or brothers or friends? How many still wandered in endless shock? Even so, the weight of the responsibilities Dina and Bernard supposedly had to the congregations was incomprehensible. The legacy of hate was indeed far-reaching.

"He could be in a grave," his mother said. "And I would hear nothing, ever. Buried — piled in a grave with others. He must be gone. I've heard nothing for so long. He would not — if he were alive, he would come —"

Elie felt taut and proud. He thought of his father as a young soldier and about the battles in Flanders, at Passchendaele. He thought of Rebbe Kishenev and his advice about ending the uncertainty. He pictured Dina's face, finally, and the look she would give him for reassurance that finding the answer was the right thing to do.

"I'm going to find out what happened to him," he assured his mother. "I'll find out."

And I'm going to win Dina, too.

SEPTEMBER 1991

Maury announced their return from the library. "Hello. We're back. Hello." The others trailed closely behind him. Hersh pushed Hannah Cohen, followed by Belinda, struggling under the books she carried.

"Oh," she said breathlessly. "I hope reading them is easier than lugging them in."

"You poor thing," Hannah said. "May I get you a glass of water? I should have taken some of those on my lap."

"No. No, thank you. Let me just get my sweater off and I'll get us all something. Do you need help with your coats?"

They were all still wearing coats. Hersh wore a black fedora and a long woolen overcoat, and while Belinda extracted herself from her knit pullover, he finally took off his hat, and helped Hannah Cohen with her wrap.

I distracted myself by concentrating on the research material they had hauled back with them to the porch. Not every title was visible from where I sat, and my view was further hampered by my efforts not to look interested. Still, I was surprised to find that I recognized most of them. There was a publication by Professor Howard M. Sachar, and though I could not see the cover, I was certain it was the renowned *The Course of Modern Jewish History*. There was also a volume on Nazi Germany, William L. Shirer's *The Rise and Fall of the Third Reich*, Elie Wiesel's *The Night Trilogy: Night, Dawn, and the Accident*, a work I had used in my classroom, and quite cleverly, I thought, an encyclopedia on the great cities of Europe, this particular volume a book of maps. Finally, there were two books that I did not recognize: *Before the Fury: Jews and Germans Before Hitler* by Emil Herz, and *The Jews of Germany* by a man named Marvin Lowenthal.

"Here's some tea. Anyone want some nice warm tea?" Belinda had changed into her uniform, and was carrying a ceramic teapot and a stack of Styrofoam cups. "I'll get the sugar and milk in a second. Sam, can you put everyone's coat over on that chair. I'll put them away later."

"So you have books," Rose said. "Anything worth telling?"

"We were very careful, like we were measuring," Hersh explained. "We knew exactly what we wanted. We got it, then we came home."

Hannah leaned toward Hersh. "We do owe our thanks to Belinda, though. After all it was her morning off. I wish we could do something nice for her."

"These books, they must have a thousand pages, each one," Harry said, after walking to the table and picking up one of the volumes. He dropped the book as if he could no longer support the tonnage. "Oye, you should enjoy these. From over there," he said, and pointed to the card table, "I'll watch you."

"Do you want some paper, Maury?" Hannah asked.

"For what do I want paper?" His eyebrows appeared to be set at a permanent angle. "I'm reading. If I want to draw pictures, then I'll get paper."

Hannah turned her attention to the others. "We're going to need to take notes on the important events we read about. How will you remember them, otherwise?"

"How do you expect me to read and take notes all at once. I only have two eyes, and two hands too. Besides, I have to hold these when I read." Maury reached into his pocket and pulled out a pair of thick bifocals, missing one earpiece. "I have to hold these with my hand. They're for reading."

"You wear glasses?" Harry muttered, "Who knew?"

"I've seen them," Gertie said, wheezing. "Not so often, because mostly he just sits."

"Can we divide these up, then?" Hersh said enthusiastically.

"Yes, let's do that and get started."

Hersh and Hannah continued to sort through the pile of books. I watched it all, confident that they were too thoroughly engaged to notice my scrutiny. When the last work had been assigned, Hersh examined the stacks. "This seems fair," he said. "Okay?"

"Good," Hannah said.

"*Oye Guttenue,*" Maury sighed, scanning the tower of books in front of him.

They read for weeks with relatively few interruptions, and I was impressed with their concentration. Secretly, I hoped these efforts would continue, since the porch was pleasantly subdued while they worked. The quiet, measured against the din of the preceding months seems almost luxurious, I wanted to tell someone. I didn't.

The skies were mostly gray outside during the days they labored at their materials, and the library-like solemnity made me daydream of rainy evenings Sarah and I had spent together in our den, reading or grading papers or preparing for the next day's classes. This tranquility, unfortunately, was not to last.

On a Sunday, near the end of the month, Elbert the

Magician made an appearance, and to my disappointment, brought with him not only his usual sleight-of-hand props but his own audience of third graders as well. Adding to my misery, the show was more insipid and clumsier than usual.

The following day, a new disturbance breached the peace, this one created by Maury's frantic public announcement. He had arrived on the porch almost breathlessly, and significantly earlier than usual. "It's Hersh," he said. He paused then, giving credence to the presumption that Hersh was dead. "It's Hersh," he repeated, nearly in tears, further fueling the fears of those waiting to hear the news. "He . . . He has escaped!"

"Who told you this news, Maury?" Harry finally asked.

"I wasn't told," he said. "I heard it."

"What is it that you heard, Maury?" Rose said.

"The nurses talking — I heard. Three times they checked his room. He never even went to his bed. Such a thing, I cannot imagine."

While I rarely felt any camaraderie with any of my neighbors, we were collectively amused by this incident. We were old, and some of us had serious physical problems, but our memories had not been so dimmed that we had forgotten the joy of intimacy. Nor had our notions of privacy been so thoroughly eroded as to require us to proclaim out loud the actual state of affairs, namely, that Samuel Hersh and Hannah Cohen were sleeping together.

Still, I did think of chiming in, following Harry's lead, and asking him whether it seemed strange that the staff was apparently unconcerned. I also wanted to add that it was very likely his two partners were not including him in every meeting regarding the project. Out of some forlorn sense of decorum, I remained quiet.

Harry, however, continued. "Do you think he made it

to the border, Maury? The F.B.I.? Have the nurses called the F.B.I.?"

Just at that moment, Hersh pushed his new roommate through the entranceway, and rolled her chair directly to their table. They seemed unaware of the gossip, but both sensed they were being observed, which was not difficult, since Margolis gaped at them in shock.

"Maury, what is it?" Hannah asked. "What's wrong?"

"I . . . I . . ." Maury said, and stopped. I believe at that instant the truth simply came to him, and he left the porch without explaining himself. For a moment, I was embarrassed for him.

The High Holy Days came late, well into autumn, and though the fast on Yom Kippur was a cause for great concern among the staff, most of those who participated survived without incident. I did not fast, not caring to have my soul cleansed as tradition dictates. In fact, in a kind of makeshift protest over my less than enviable circumstances, I ate defiantly.

Inevitably, just after Yom Kippur, Maury Margolis' enthusiasm for the project began to fade. He had slept through many of the afternoons during the holidays, with his book in his lap, but one day rather suddenly, and without cause, he awoke from his midday drowsiness. "Oye," he sighed. He looked toward Hannah to gauge her reaction, but there was none. I went back to my book, but when I looked up again, a moment later, it was clear he was struggling.

I was amazed. He had persevered longer than I had thought possible, a feat I attributed to his teaching background. "Oh, please, this is awful," he said, looking up once more.

"Maury?" Hersh finally said.

"Would you like a different book?" Hannah asked.

Margolis put down his glasses and rubbed his eyes. "It is very hard work," she said, and then tried to console him by rubbing his hand.

"Maury, you're tired," Hersh said. "But we all —"

"If I were just tired, that would be all right. I wouldn't be such a nudge," Margolis said. "I don't know about you, but my eyes hurt, my wrist hurts from turning, turning and turning, even my lap hurts. These books are like stones."

This was the first time I could recall anyone claiming his energy had been sapped by the effort of turning pages.

"Couldn't we just make it simple," he said. "One day I'm going to wake up and find out I died from overreading."

Hannah grinned. "No one ever died from reading,"

"You say no, but this reading, it's like going to your own funeral. You could die from it. We could be buried and we'd never even know we were gone."

"You were a teacher." Hannah said. "You —"

"I taught math. Math!" Margolis put his hands over his ears. "Math. That's all. All right, a little science, too. But I just can't do this anymore. I'm wasting away into nothing here. We should stop. Enough already." He became calmer as his resolve to quit became public, and, finally, he slumped down in silence.

"We can help you, Maury," Hannah said.

"Why don't you just rest this afternoon?" Belinda said. "You'll feel better in the morning. Come on, I'll get someone to help you to your room. You can lay down for a while."

"Perhaps tomorrow," he said. "Oye, tomorrow again."

• • •

Maury did return to the porch, but he did not rejoin Hersh and Hannah and did not volunteer any more of his time to their endeavor. Over the next days he moved from table to table trying to reclaim a space for himself, and Hersh and

Hannah Cohen, though they made efforts to rekindle his enthusiasm, finally relented and left him alone.

Over the next weeks, I continued to monitor them periodically as the pace of their reading and research accelerated. They discussed with wonder each of the battles they studied from World War I, and many of the events leading to the Holocaust. A battle at Passchendaele in the fall of 1916, held their attention for a number of days. The politics of the early days of Nazi Germany also intrigued them, and, for perhaps a week, they traded facts back and forth regarding the laws that had been enacted and proclamations regarding the status of Jews in the doomed community.

"I could read for a thousand years and still I — How could it happen?" I heard Hannah say to Hersh one afternoon.

Tears were streaming down her cheeks.

APRIL 1948

Elie entered the building, his heart pounding.

"And your name is?" a woman inquired.

"I'm Elie Wasserman. I'm looking for Frana Luftwantz."

The service run by Frana Luftwantz had been relocated by the city to an abandoned warehouse. The height of the ceilings and the emptiness made the office, tucked in one far corner, appear small and out of place. Also, as there were no walls or dividers separating the volunteers to Elie there appeared to be an aimless milling about. The overhead lights further contributed to the dreariness. Bare bulbs hung from wires tied to the ceiling's iron rafters and the breeze from open transoms made these makeshift fixtures sway, so that strange shadows fell over everyone.

"You'll have to wait," she said. "There are chairs near the door." Elie turned. "Sorry, it's so cold and dim in here. This is all the city would give us. They told us if we were cold to wear sweaters."

There was an older Hassidic man rubbing the tallises on his tzitzit, and another man in clothes smudged with grease, his head lowered. An entire family sat huddled at the far end.

"Okay," Elie said, but the woman had already reached the door and was bending over the man in the dirty overalls.

Elie sat near the Hassidic man. Would Bernard be kind to Dina, he wondered. He didn't know Rabbi Liebenshul's son, but he imagined him as distant. Bernard's father had a reputation of being rigid and unfriendly. Elie worried that the son was likely to be the same. Dina will be miserable if he won't talk to her, he thought.

"I've seen many faces in these chairs," the Hassidic man declared. "Yours, I have not seen."

Elie did not feel like talking.

The man adjusted his *shtreimel*. "These chairs, they were once filled. From morning until night, always. And the faces here, they were all damp with sadness. A room full of tears. Every day, the same. Not these chairs exactly, of course. This is when the office was run by the Khal Anshei Chessed. When the war was over, there were so many here, you would have to stand for hours before they even took your name. Some would come and stay all day, crying all the time. Children, women looking for husbands. It seemed to me as if everyone in the world must be looking for someone."

Elie was curious. "Are you looking for someone? Have you been looking all this time?"

"My name is Lazar Poliakoff. And may I ask who you are?"

"Elie Wasserman. Do you mind me asking that question? I mean you don't have to tell me. I'd understand, I promise."

"I'm pleased to meet you. Under the circumstances, a different place would have been better, but I'm glad we met nevertheless. Tell me first, am I correct? Have I seen you here before?

"I came today for the first time. I wrote a letter to someone named Frana Luftwantz a few weeks ago. She wrote back and told me to come today."

"Frana, she is an important woman here. Without her, I think we would all live in darkness forever."

"Rebbe Kishenev told me I should see her. He said —"

"Do you pray at Adas Yeraim?"

"We attend Ohab Zedek. I was —"

"That you call praying? Do they still teach the Talmud there or have they forsaken the Talmud too? Eh, I'm just saying. Do not listen to me."

"Rebbe Kishenev —"

"If you pray at Ohab Zedek, how do you know Rebbe Kishenev? This much you can tell me, please. Is the rebbe talking about his plan to bring the congregations together, even over at Ohab Zedek? Is that what's happening? He's like the mayor that one. Shaking hands instead of studying the Talmud. He should teach his congregation the Talmud. Leave the rest to God to take care of."

"No, no, he hasn't been at Ohab Zedek. That isn't how I know him."

"Oh?"

"I . . . I know Dina Kishenev, his daughter. I met her one day. By accident."

"By accident? How do you meet someone by accident?"

"I . . . well I was playing in a basketball game."

"Ah yes," Lazer nodded. "I've heard this. So you're the one."

"I'm the one."

"She has recovered?"

"Yes, she's fine," Elie said.

"Good. Where are you from? May I ask this also?"

"I was born in Freiburg. It's a city in southern Germany."

"I am familiar with this place. I know of it. I'm told that before the war it was lovely. Many Jews lived there. I believe I'm correct about this? And when did you arrive here, in Mattapan? Before the war? You must have been young. You speak as if you have lived here always."

Elie considered telling Lazar Poliakoff the history of their trip to America, but he was distracted by a volunteer who had come to speak to the family waiting in the nearby chairs.

"Are you looking for someone?" Elie asked Poliakof. "It's none of my business, so you don't have to tell me, if you don't want to."

The woman in the family began to cry.

"I first came here to learn about my brother and his four children. They lived in a shtetel in Russia, in Minsk. This was a man so gentle he would not fight the wind on his walk home from shul."

"You've been waiting all this time?"

"No, my brother worked at Balzec for three years before he was shot for giving his potato to a child. A quarter of a potato, uncooked. His children were murdered in the showers at Treblinka. My brother's wife, Resse, I learned last year she had bad teeth, a mouth full of gold fillings. She died from bleeding. Nothing to stop the pain of the bleeding when they pulled these teeth out. The whole family is gone."

"If you already know what happened to them, why do you still come?"

"Today, I have brought a friend. From Austria he has come. He is looking for his daughter," Lazar said. "But I'm thinking this may have been a mistake."

"A mistake?" Elie asked.

"The families, the ones that came even before the war was over, these people they understood. They came knowing what they would find out. They came because they had to know. Because they had to have the fear end." He raised his eyes. He was looking for his friend, Elie thought "They can say the Kaddish and the pain, at least most of it, will go away and leave the memories to linger behind. That is our way. But my friend, he is waiting for a miracle from God. He came for instructions. For a map to find the place where his daughter is waiting for him. He knows the truth but he does not know. I'm worried that he's like his daughter, lost forever. That's why a mistake this might be."

Elie thought of his mother sitting on the sofa night after night listening to the radio and waiting.

"Do you understand what you're looking for?" Poliakoff asked. "What you will find out here, it may not be — Ah, this is none of my business."

"No, no, I understand," Elie said. "I . . . My mother . . . We . . ." He could not come up with words.

"You are a brave boy." Poliakoff placed a hand on Elie's knee and prayed for him.

Elie's hoped some of his father's bravery was indeed in him.

"Eh, you may speak. Speak, young lady. You apparently have something to say to this young man here. Come." Lazar spoke over Elie's shoulder. "I believe he'll listen to you."

Elie realized his acquaintance was addressing someone behind him.

"Hi," she said. Elie turned. He thought he had seen her before, but he couldn't remember her name. She had a young boy with her whose hand she gripped tightly.

"Well," Lazar groused, "what is it? It will be difficult, indeed, if you don't say more than you have said."

Elie guessed she was about his own age, maybe he had seen her in the store or at Hecht House. Her scarf tied back behind her ears covered a mop of red hair, and her skin was dark and freckled. The boy had similar features.

"Hi," Elie responded.

"We have never been formally introduced," Poliakoff said. "But I believe you are the daughter of Nahum Moscow. The baker. Is this right? I need to know no more about you than that to say I am pleased to meet you. Your name, however, would be nice to learn."

"I'm Naomi Moscow. And this is my brother, Ben." She lifted their hands. "I . . . I'm a friend of Dina's — Dina Kishenev?"

Elie's heart jumped, then he felt unnerved.

"I am Lazar Poliakoff. I am also leaving. The conversation I think you are about to have does not require the presence of an old man."

"Do you mind that I came here?" Naomi asked. "I had to bring Ben. Mother won't let me go anywhere without someone with me. She says the Irish boys in the Square might like my red hair."

Before he could reassure her, Elie heard his name called. "How did you know I'd be here?" Curiosity swarmed him and he was torn between answering the woman beckoning him and demanding that Naomi explain her presence.

"I went to Isaac Gurlock's store, near my father's shop. He said you'd be here. Isaac, that is. He and my father are friends. Dina told me to find you at Isaac's, but you weren't there so I came here. What is this place? It's so dark."

The woman called to Elie again, louder this time. "How did you know who I was?"

"I just knew."

"Elie Wasserman, Elie Wasserman." Elie got up to answer.

"I'm Dina's friend. She wanted me to tell you something."

"Elie, please, others are waiting."

"Okay. Can you wait here? Wait here, all right?

"My name is Shana." Elie greeted a pale woman with a small nose reddened by a cold. He teeth were crooked and her hair disheveled, but her eyes were gray and kind. "I'm going to take you to Mrs. Arbiter. You haven't been here before, looking? It's difficult, I know. Mrs. Arbiter, she will help you if she can."

They stopped at a desk cluttered with papers. "Mrs. Arbiter, this is Elie — Elie Wasserman." Mrs. Arbiter stood straight and somewhat rigidly as she shook Elie's hand. Her clothes were pressed and impeccable; her face a mixture of exhaustion and seriousness.

"I wrote to Frana Luftwantz about two weeks ago," Elie said. "I'm . . ." He felt as though he could not speak. "I'm looking for my father."

"I have your letter right here. Your father's name is Emil Wasserman, as I recall. You came from Freiburg. Your father was a journalist and he stayed in Germany after you left in 1933. You and your mother went through several European refugee camps and finally traveled from England to Canada to Chicago, and eventually, to Mattapan. You, or at least your mother, was able to maintain some contact with your father by post until about the time of Krystalnacht, 1938. After that, the letters stopped. Why have you waited all these years, Elie? Your mother has not been here before, either. It's been such a long time."

Elie thought about what he should say. He wanted to tell her that all of his memories were of expectation. He wanted to explain that he had always heard that his father would one day walk through the door, from the time when he was too young to have doubts. At seventeen, he felt very old. "I should've come sooner. I don't really remember my father, I was very small when we left. My mother still waits for my father to walk through the door. At least she did until recently." Around him Elie could see rows of files all marked: PROPERTY OF THE UNITED STATES. The files were military green and Elie guessed they had been transported from Europe and that they contained information on the lost and the dead.

"She needs to know now," Elie continued. "She's still young. I want her to get her life back from the war."

Mrs. Arbiter nodded as if she had heard this before.

"Did you find out what happened to him? You remember my letter so well."

Her smile disappeared. Mrs. Arbiter turned to face her desk and laid her hands across the files there. "The Nazis, they were not just evil, you see, they were also desperate people and cowards. Miserable cowards. All of which makes for a very frightening combination. They were the killers of the innocent and the weak, women and children, babies, in the name of a policy that they proclaimed was moral and noble. They said that it was God's will to do this." To Elie she looked as if she might spit on the floor. "But when it came time to face the truth, to tell all of their policy, of their morality, and let the world judge their choice to purify their people — well, then, like frightened cowards, they couldn't even utter the words to describe what they'd done, or tried to do. We have no policy of genocide, they lied. And worse, they did what they could to destroy their own records. To hide what they had done in the name of their hideous natural law."

"I understand, but —"

"Let me finish, Elie. I don't mean to lecture you. I know you know how terrible these people were. Forgive me. The point is, they destroyed so much of their records, it's difficult to locate someone or even to know what happened to them. We've done our best. We've spoken to the survivors from the camps and tried to get the names of everyone that we could — dead and alive. The survivors were our best source. The Germans, they did not wait for us to read through their documents. Many of the records near the end of the war were burned in the same ovens they —" She sighed, and to Elie it seemed she might be nauseous. "I'm sorry. Frana would not like my attitude today."

Elie began to worry that they had found nothing. Mrs. Arbiter's inflection was not encouraging.

"There were rumors during the early part of the war, about what was going on. Then, later, witnesses. The Nazis did not want anyone to know, so they eliminated as much evidence as they could. Himmler, he did everything he could to hide his crimes. He — Paul Biobel the kommandant — had his soldiers dig up the mass grave at Chelmno. Jews, they had been shot there. Thousands, in lines, shot down. Women, children, and then buried in a mass grave." She put her fingers to her lips. "Himmler heard there had been witnesses. So he ordered his men to dig up the grave, uncover the bodies they had left there, and then they poured kerosene over the dead and burned them into ashes."

Elie filled with a confluence of rage and terror. Was his father killed this way? He would have fought them, he thought.

"This is how methodical they were about their guilt," Mrs. Arbiter said. "These were evil men."

There was silence between them. Even through his wrath, Elie was glad his mother had not come to hear this. She was not strong enough. "I think you're telling me you can't find my father. That you don't know what happened to him. Is that it?"

Her shoulders slumped. "For several weeks we've had your letter. All of our sources we've tried. People who were in camps who came from Freiburg. Even people who came from nearby towns. We've searched through whatever records there are. But we've found nothing. You should tell your mother that some who survived, even though there are not many from Freiburg, they are settling in Palestine."

"I will. But —"

"We can't find him, Elie. We'll keep trying. Emil Wasserman. There seems to be no one who can give us information about his fate."

Elie felt unsteady. His mouth was dry. "Does that mean he wasn't in a camp — your not having any information, I mean? Would you know it if he'd been in such a place?"

"I just don't know. People were starving in these camps; their memories were not perfect. Even those we spoke to, some remember so little of the details. Most were near death for years. Your father, Elie, he could have been with them, sleeping next to them on the racks, and they may never have known him. I wish I had more for you. I can only promise we'll continue to look."

Desperation wrapped around Elie. "Please tell me one thing. And please tell me the truth. Is it possible? Could he turn up in some city somewhere, looking for us? Or in Israel? Somewhere? Anywhere? I just need to know what to tell my mother. I met a man out by the door who was certain too much time had passed. He was certain my father was gone. That he was dead."

"People must make their own peace," she said. "In God's eyes anything is possible. I will — we should leave it in his good hands."

"Thank you," Elie said. "I understand."

"There is one question I need to ask you before you go. It may help us, and it is something people sometimes forget to mention. Sometimes when people first came to this country, they changed their names. Either they thought they were too hard to pronounce, or the immigration official thought so, so the name was changed. Fitka became Frank. Golinsky became Gold. Do you understand what I'm asking? Was there another name? Is it possible that we are checking the wrong name?"

"No, it was always Wasserman. In Freiburg and here. The spelling is the same too. It wasn't changed."

"Was Emil your father's formal name? Could it have been something he didn't like so he used another name? Was it a middle name perhaps and he had a different first name? A nickname, perhaps? Something else he was called?"

"No. It was Emil Wasserman. That's all. Emil Wasserman. That was his name."

"I'm sorry. I wish there were more I could tell you. I thought perhaps we were checking the wrong name. That could have been something, anyway." Mrs. Arbiter stood and shook Elie's hand. "Good-bye, Elie. If I hear anything at all, I'll contact you. I have your address."

"Thank you again for your help." He could see Naomi Moscow reading to her brother and he remembered she was waiting for him. He crossed the drafty expanse and sat down beside her. Naomi closed her book.

"Can we go now?" Ben asked impatiently. "Morris Reif is waiting for me. He's got a real baseball."

"In a minute, Ben."

"Where do you live?" Elie asked.

"On Evelyn Street" Naomi replied. "Near the shul. That's how I know the Kishenevs. I mean I know the rebbe because we attend Adas Yeraim. But Dina is my friend also."

"It's okay. I'll walk you home. On the way you can tell me why you came here."

They walked into the chilly air, but Naomi seemed reluctant to say anything more.

"It's okay," Elie said. "You can tell me. It's okay."

"Dina told me to tell you that she loves Bernard," Naomi said. "That she loves him and she wants to marry him. She said she wasn't clear when she was with you before. She didn't want you to think she wasn't in love with Bernard. She said she is, and to tell you that. To make it clear so you would forget about her. You confused her about Bernard just for a minute but she understands now what she needs to do."

Elie was sure the words were hollow, but they hurt. "Why didn't she come to tell me these things herself?"

"Uh. She couldn't . . .Um, there wasn't . . . I was supposed to be . . . She said that she couldn't look at you and say the words. She thought she would cry, and that she didn't want to cry in front of you. I was not supposed to tell you that."

Elie wondered whether his father was watching over him. He felt as if he needed someone to help him, but he was not sure how.

"I should go. My parents will want me to get Ben home."

"Okay."

"You don't have to walk with us. Our house is not so far. I walk with Ben all the time by ourselves," she said. "Oh, there is one more thing. Dina said to tell you that she hoped you would find your father." She grabbed her brother's hand. "She wanted you to know that she thinks he was a hero."

Elie turned to look toward the service offices. "What did you say?"

"What do you mean?"

"You said Dina hoped I'd find my father, and —"

"That she thought he was a hero."

"I have to go. Are you sure you'll be okay?"

"Of course, but —"

"Thanks." He was already running toward the agency and Mrs. Arbiter.

NOVEMBER 1991

In contrast to my stark quarters, the other residents personalized their rooms, often creating altars to their former lives.

Gertie Neustadt, in addition to the baskets of yarn strewn about and the sewing machine that stood prominently by the window, displayed a tattered wedding gown on a mannequin, and patent leather shoes, which were tacked to the wall. Below the dress sat several photographs and an engraved wedding invitation in a frame, circled by dried flowers.

Harry's room was nearly identical to Gertie's, though in his, a knobby football rested at an angle on a wooden stand, surrounded by albums overflowing with news clippings. The ball had an inscription, but it had faded from the leather. The stitching was also unraveling, and the laces were frayed but there was no doubt, this was a trophy of sorts.

Perhaps the most remarkable quarters belonged to Dr. Nathan. His room was barren of furniture and similar to mine, except that he had made the meticulous effort of cutting out the pages of *The Physicians' Guidebook of 1958,* and taping the text to his walls. He had also detached the photographs of anatomical malformations, and had Belinda enlarge them at the copy machine before exhibiting them as well. This turned the room into an eerie and macabre museum, and made me certain he was insane.

In contrast to Dr. Nathan's shrine to the medical sciences, Rose Goodman's quarters appeared to be a gallery of religious art. On her walls hung several faded paintings — all signed R. Goodman — portraying scenes from the Torah. There was one in particular that drew my eye. Abraham, standing on the mount, gazing up to God with agony on his face as he raised a knife over his son Isaac. I didn't know whether I was surprised at the quality of the work and was envious of her talents, or whether I just loathed the story of God commanding Abraham to kill his son. Either way, I was always quick to look away.

The one room that seemed to break the mold, predictably, belonged to Hersh. It was nearest to the porch and oddly hexagonal, but was different, not only because of the shape, but because there was activity inside, which, over time, became notorious throughout the home. Hersh and Hannah Cohen spent every night there, huddled, working on their story.

Hersh was the first to arrive on the porch each morning; I knew this because I generally followed closely behind him. He was an earlier riser than his new roommate, though it might have been that they rose together and she then went to physical therapy; a morning routine I had long ago discarded. In any event, I felt, in the mornings, as if Hersh wanted me to greet him; that he wanted me to ask how it was going, and each morning he watched the door as I arrived and followed my movements until I settled down to read.

"What are you staring at?" I would say to him. And he would just turn away or say something inane such as: "I'm not staring. I'm thinking." I believe we reached an understanding at some point. Our dialogue became a familiar dawn ritual.

Soon after he and Hannah had reached agreement on the story line, they moved some distance away from me. I suppose I could have been offended, but I was sure they didn't move because of my eavesdropping or because of my nasty demeanor. Instead, it appeared they changed tables to be closer to where Mrs. Silver sat, and, in fact, they spent almost a month gathering information from the poor woman regarding her past.

It was interesting to witness the interrogations. Hersh sometimes read from a list of questions while Hannah took notes. Belinda stood guard over her patient, and frowned when Hersh went too fast or asked a question that she thought might agitate the woman in physical decline. The process seemed misguided to me. They were ultimately going to disappoint Mrs. Silver either with their sure-to-be clumsy reprise of her story, or by abandoning her once they had the testimony they needed.

From the bits of conversation I could hear during their probing, it was clear that they covered a wide array of subjects with the endlessly patient woman, and to their credit, they covered topics that piqued Mrs. Silver's interest, while serving their own needs as well. They spent several days looking at a map of Freiburg in the encyclopedia, and Mrs. Silver pointed out streets she knew. That discussion led her to a discourse on her childhood, and a biographical essay on her duties as the daughter of an Orthodox shoemaker. This was followed by a tearful description of the death of her father. She also described *Der Shürmer,* the vicious anti-Semitic newspaper, and the attitudes of merchants and shopkeepers who once were her friends but who came to look at her as the cause of their ills. And, finally, she told of candlelight debates with her husband, Albert, about his role as a former war hero and, accordingly, about his responsibilities to his fellow Jews under the new regime.

Eventually, after many days, they apparently obtained

all that they felt they needed and explained to Mrs. Silver that they would have to move on. They did ask her to help with the outlining and the writing, but she politely declined. I realized, to my surprise, that the process had been therapeutic for Mrs. Silver, in spite of its necessary conclusion. Her posture seemed sturdier and her face glowed. I was displeased, of course, but not because she seemed to feel better. No, I was afraid that Belinda would notice the change and force us into some kind of group sessions where we all described our youths, in an effort to restore our vitality. I'm not sure why this was a concern. Without qualms, I would have simply refused.

The table Hersh and Hannah had chosen as their own for the work of outlining and writing — at least during the day — was on the other side of the porch, as far from me as possible. This location was also a considerable distance from Maury, who clearly found their decision to change tables conspiratorial. To everyone's dismay, he became vocal about their treason, and he complained that their affair was the cause of his own inability to contribute.

The project had attained a kind of celebrity. Hersh and Hannah were bombarded with requests for updates on the story line at meals, and when they stopped for tea or to rest their eyes, questions cascaded down upon them.

From what I could piece together, the outlining proceeded smoothly, and, to their credit, the actual document appeared to be carefully detailed. They had gone back to Mrs. Silver at intervals during the process to clarify or to ensure the accuracy of her story. To my surprise, they spent several afternoons with the rabbi of Emunah to discuss intricacies of Talmudic requirements. I attributed most of the credit for the finished skeleton draft to Hannah Cohen. Her organizational skill was remarkable. Each category had been exhaustively inventoried with mountainous notes and then labeled, with a cover sheet and a table of contents, and the outline itself was tabbed into chapters and sub-tabbed by paragraph.

"That's brilliant," Hersh would call out repeatedly, or "Very good, yes, I like that." His exclamation would be followed by a kiss to indicate his amazement at her originality, and her ability to concentrate.

Their interaction was much like mine and Sarah's, years earlier. I sensed that he was in awe of Hannah Cohen; nearly mesmerized by her, just as I had been by Sarah. Please don't think about it, I urged myself silently. But the similarities were plain. Often, as I watched them, I was overwhelmed with despondency.

As for their story, it underwent some minor changes as they proceeded, which I deduced from fragments of the conversations I overheard.

The setting, I knew, was moved from Brooklyn to Mattapan, and certain characters were transformed, and others created, as they proceeded.

"Dina's full of hopes and dreams," I heard Hannah Cohen say, as they passed my chair one afternoon, "but she's devoted to her father, and we have to let her be as she is even though I don't think Bea, under the circumstances, would have been quite as loyal." This character had taken on a persona of her own. I had read of authors who believed that, once established, the temperaments of those that populated their works were independent of their control; that often the writer was surprised by something his creation did or said. My interest, of course, was not so much that this occurred, but rather that these novices had experienced this phenomenon.

They also began a public forum on names one afternoon, and discussed the propriety of certain monikers at length.

"A German immigrant? Solomon?" Harry contributed. "That sounds like the name of one of Saulie's friends from the G & G Deli."

"The Deli has been closed for years," Hersh replied.

"It has to have a German sound and be a Jewish name," Hannah Cohen instructed them. "This is a man who fought for Germany in the First War and then immigrated, and who can still speak of his earlier years in Germany as if he misses them. Someone who knew the father." Then this character was not part of the original story; at least not as I remembered from Mrs. Silver's tale. I guessed that the character's function was a segue; a bridge perhaps from their boy protagonist to the object of his search, his lost father.

"Menachem Begin," Maury shouted out.

"Jergen something?" Hersh offered. "What do you think?"

There was no response. I believe they would have remained stuck had Belinda not rescued them with a telephone book. "Pick one from this list," she said, "the right name is in there somewhere."

Once, I had pored over the phonebook, searching for the right names for my characters, and to relieve me of the responsibility of creating personalities for them. I finally took names from the obituary page, and for a brief moment I considered offering the suggestion to Hersh.

"Here it is," Hersh called out, leafing through the phonebook. "Kultz."

"Kultz?" Belinda asked. "That's a name?"

"Something Kultz? I don't know," Hersh said. "To me Kultz sounds German. How about Menachem Kultz?"

One part of the story that did not change was the ending. I knew this, because they discussed it openly and often. There was no doubt about the couple's devotion to optimism and their desire to resolve each story line with a happy finale. What was unforeseen, however, was their need to engage in a public dialogue regarding the details of the denouement. Obviously, they sought approval.

"Dina and Elie must be married," Hannah Cohen repeated.

"And the father must be found, alive, and able to tell his story," Hersh added.

"I'll be so thrilled to read a book with a happy ending," Belinda said. "Finally some writers with sense."

I grew tired of all of it. They are going to outline forever, I thought. They will never actually begin to write. After all, that's when it usually fails.

But, the outlining did eventually give way to the writing, and though I anticipated disagreement and infighting, there was never an instance when they were anything other than enchanted. They composed and they laughed. They wrote and then looked at each other as if they had, together, made a grand discovery. Around them people delighted in their happiness and their sense of purpose. "This is wonderful," Rose announced each afternoon as they nuzzled together. "This is so wonderful, what you are doing." And later, as some would drift back toward their rooms, they rubbed Hersh on his back as they passed.

"Mazel Tov. The Pulitzer. That's for you, Hannah Cohen," an orderly said one day.

"This Pulitzer, he was Jewish? Myron Pulitzer, no?" Maury asked.

Perhaps three weeks after the actual drafting began, Stubs, the orderly, waddled his way onto the porch shoving a stainless-steel food cart laden with large cardboard boxes.

"What is it?" Hersh asked, glancing up.

"Harry?" Stubs called out.

"Ech, what the hell is it? I'm busy," Harry grumbled from the card table.

Stubs turned to Hannah Cohen. "Harry thought you might need this," he announced. "He asked me if I'd bring it in today."

Hannah glanced over toward Harry, who did not acknowledge her. "What is it, exactly?"

"It's a computer. Well, it's really a computer with some software that does word processing. You know what I mean?"

"No, we have no idea what you mean," Hersh responded. "This we wouldn't possibly be able to use. Please, take it back."

"Does it have instructions?" Hannah asked.

"Of course it has Goddamn instructions," Harry cursed. "Get the Goddamn instructions out of the box. What are you, a shmuck? Open the box. Get out the instructions. What are you looking at, Hersh?"

"Is this a gift, Harry?" Belinda exclaimed. "Well, I'll be."

"Isn't that nice," Rose said. "What a lovely thing to do."

"Harry, you old softy," Hersh said with a huge grin. "I didn't think you had it in you."

"Enough of this horseshit," Harry declared. "It was Stubs's idea, the whole thing."

"What are you talking about?" Stubs blurted. "I still have your check, right here. Shut up and open the box. You talk too much. Just like the rest."

Hannah Cohen spent the next hour enthralled as Stubs opened each box and placed each component on the table in front of her, and she was absolutely in awe as he configured the pieces and connected the tangle of wires at the back.

"This thing, Mrs. Cohen, what does it do?" Maury asked.

"That is quite obviously a computer," Dr. Nathan

declared dryly, as he walked onto the porch, having missed the earlier conversation.

"What? You can't mind your own business?" Maury shouted. "I know what it is, I asked what it does."

The machine could edit text, had a dictionary and a thesaurus, and could check spelling. I had no idea, nor did I learn from listening to the questions, how the machine was made to do these things, but I was impressed. If I had a computer when I'd made my attempt at a novel, I thought, I might not have given up.

I couldn't believe they were better able to write a novel, particularly at their age, than I had been in my youth, and I watched for the patterns I recalled from my own failed attempts. I studied them for signs of depression, lethargy, melancholy, idleness. I waited for them to take time off; to declare themselves too tired to continue or too involved with the story; to say that they needed to get some distance. I listened for excuses not to sit at the machine; to clean or organize or socialize. I poised myself for arguments; petty disputes that I was sure would come. And finally, I waited for them to decide their story was just not good enough.

As I observed their efforts, my own frailties were, again, vividly exposed. Perhaps I didn't really like to write, or I did not have either the ability or the tenacity to compose anything worthwhile; that I would be found to be little more than a dreamer; someone never committed to anything, and not really worth very much. I decided that I was lucky in a way, that Sarah could not have children. I would have made a mess of that too. If you want to be a writer, then sit and write, people would say. I repeated the phrase almost daily in my head. I knew it was true. I could never do it.

Hersh and Hannah appeared to have an inexhaustible

supply of energy and an unfailing desire to work. Distractions were ignored; boredom never did set in. Certainly, they were stalled on occasion, no one could deny that. But they did what I never could do when the going became difficult; they worked harder.

"We will stagger our way through it," I heard Hannah say, on one occasion, after they had sat without progress for perhaps half a day. And by those words alone they seemed to regain momentum. "If it takes us thirty years, we'll sit here until we get it the way we want," Hersh declared once, and I recognized that failure had very little to do with lack of ability. I failed because I was lazy. Nothing more than a fool. Thank God Sarah isn't here, I thought.

Some three months later, near the end of March, I eavesdropped on a conversation between them that was meant to be private.

"This is absolutely wonderful," Hersh said, as I passed the door to his room. I knew I should move on, but I stayed to listen. "One chapter to go. It's hard to believe we've come this far."

"I'm so proud of us" Hannah agreed. "Sometimes, when I think about what we've accomplished, I wonder how did we have the energy. How in God's name were we ever able to focus on this, as we promised? The odds were not in our favor."

Hersh chuckled. "I suppose not. You pulled me along."

"I don't think so. We worked because we liked being with one another. But there was something else too."

"You'd have come around to it by yourself, eventually. You didn't really need help from me. This I know."

"I did need your help," she said. "But what I'm talking about is different. When I sit at the typewriter, when I'm writing away, sometimes I get lost. It's almost as if I'm transformed into one of the characters inside the story, as though I were Dina or Elie, feeling exactly what they're feeling. I have conversations, their conversations. I'm twenty years old and in love and living out a wonderful drama that I already know will have a wonderful conclusion. It's like having another life."

Hersh was quiet.

"You've let me feel what it's like to be young again. Free of this chair. I'm proud of the book. I'm proud of how hard we have worked so far. But I was dying before you arrived. I missed the world so much. I love you for that more than you'll ever know. I don't think I have ever been happier."

I rolled away, hoping that they wouldn't hear me.

That night I lay awake many hours thinking about Sarah.

"Honey, will you go get us a soda," Sarah said to me at the South End Pottery Show. "The stand is across the grounds, over behind those other booths. Do you see it? Over there?" She pointed to a Coca-Cola sign in the distance.

"Yes, no problem," I said. I was glad to have something to do other than mill about her friend's booth, which hadn't drawn a customer all afternoon.

I was halfway across, wending my way through the crowd.

"Abe." I heard Sarah shout excitedly. "Abe, Abe over here." She was yelling, and I turned, confused. She was jumping and waving at me to approach and everyone was staring, wondering what the fuss was about. "You have to see this woman's work over here." She pointed at her friend's bowls and plates, then picked one up and held it for the

crowd to see. "It's the best in the whole show! You have to come see it. Hurry! There won't be anything left."

"Did you really want a soda?" I said later watching the crowd hovering over her friend's tables.

"No. But thanks for going to get one for me."

MAY 1948

Elie was out of breath as he ran into the agency. His mouth was dry and he trembled from nervousness. He closed his eyes, said a prayer, and looked at the chair where he had first met Lazar Poliakoff a week earlier. "I hope your friend found his family," he said to the empty seat.

"Elie," Mrs. Arbiter called from the distance. "Elie," she waved at him.

Elie was not sure he could move. He felt rigid with tension at what he might hear. Be strong, he thought, for my father.

"Come in. Come," Mrs. Arbiter said, holding his arm. "*Der Hebraish Held,* who would have thought? Amazing."

Elie found several people there waiting for him.

"You can sit, it's all right," Mrs. Arbiter said. "This is Avi Pilson," she pointed to a stout man standing behind her chair. "And this is Captain Chamberlain, Grear Chamberlain." Captain Chamberlain wore his army dress uniform, a black tunic with brass buttons and ribbons on his lapel. "Captain Chamberlain is a doctor. He is with the Veterans Administration — The army. Mr. Pilson is an archivist. They are both from Chicago. They help us from time to time."

Elie was certain that these people knew something. "My father is dead, isn't he?"

"Did you bring the picture of your father?" Avi Pilson asked.

Elie lifted the frame from his pocket and handed it to him.

"Your father was a journalist? Is that correct?" Mrs. Arbiter asked. Pilson handed the photograph to Captain Chamberlain.

"Yes," he answered impatiently. "Why do you need a picture of him? Is he dead? Have you found records?"

"Oye, you're going too fast," Mrs. Arbiter pleaded. "Please."

"Please tell me what you know. It's all right. I'll be all right."

"We have a lot to tell you," Avi Pilson said. "You need to listen."

"Either he's dead or he's not." Elie stared at them.

"There were a lot of stories to search though about *Der Hebraish Held*," Mrs. Arbiter said. "That is why we were so surprised when you came back that day. We couldn't believe it. We had always assumed that the name meant Hero to the Hebrews. That it referred to a non-Jew. It had to be a German, someone with a position in the community, someone who needed to protect himself. There were many families, survivors, who gave credit to this man for their lives."

"Many families? What do you mean many families?" Elie frantically wanted information.

"Families were told by intermediaries to gather, always in the middle of the night, sometimes behind a beer hall or in an alley. Sometimes in Freiburg. Sometimes in Ravensburg. Sometimes in Memmingen. Jewish families were disappearing and being sent to camps."

Elie watched Chamberlain peer at his father's picture.

"Only families of three could go. That is what they were told. There was no room for anyone else in the vehicle. Only three. Sometimes it was the mother and two children. Sometimes a family with only one child. Sometimes it was only the children. Only three could go."

"They were blindfolded," Avi Pilson interrupted, "then told to wait. If the blindfolds were removed, they were told the vehicle would pull away and their opportunity would be lost. When the vehicle came, they were put beneath the floorboards, in a hidden compartment and told to remain still and quiet. For several hours they were driven to the border. The driver used a journalist's pass to get them across. Several of the people who escaped heard the guards complaining that journalists created more work for them. That is how we know he used a journalist's pass."

"They were dropped off with a relief group in Switzerland, in Zurich," Mrs. Arbiter continued. "They were held in safety until the end of the war. That is when we began to hear these stories. No one," she explained, "spoke of this before the end of the war for fear of exposing this man somehow. Everyone kept quiet. That is why I asked about whether he worked as a reporter."

Elie studied them. He was confused about what they were telling him and frustrated they did not get to the point, but he also felt proud. "He was banned by the law from the paper he worked at because he was Jewish. He could not have had papers like that."

"No," Mrs. Arbiter responded, "but he was likely to have been one of the last Jewish journalists to have retained his papers before the government policy came into effect banning Jews. For a while, at least, they made exceptions for those Jewish men who had served at the front in World War I. For a while, if you had served, you could still work."

"How old is this picture?" Chamberlain asked.

Elie wanted to scream. "Tell me —"

"We decided to look in Chicago," Mrs. Arbiter broke in. "Your mother's last letters were sent from Chicago. We decided to start there. If he somehow survived or avoided the camps, or even if he was eventually put into a camp, we decided we should continue as if he had lived. If he did, what would he do? We asked ourselves, where would he go? Back to Freiburg? We did not think so. To Palestine maybe? Maybe, but we thought not. We decided that what he was likely to do was to make his way to Chicago, if he could. To see if he could find you."

"There is a man," Dr. Chamberlain said. "He is very sick, but he is alive. He is in a hospital in Chicago. A veterans' hospital there called the Cabrini V.A. Hospital."

Elie thought he might be imagining what he just heard.

"I don't know for sure who this man is. I wish that I did." Chamberlain pulled a file from the edge of the desk. "He's not well. His heart is very weak. He was at Treblinka for a time, but we don't know for certain how long. The number's in sequence with those from Treblinka. I'm trying to find out more."

Elie felt as if he were underwater; as if he hadn't taken a breath in hours and his senses were blurred

"He should know the rest," Avi Pilson said, glaring at the doctor.

"The man we're talking about has no identification or at least he didn't have any with him when he was brought to the hospital. He was brought to the Veterans' because, when he drifted into consciousness, he seemed to know certain military information. He would awaken, and, at random, describe the positions of certain regiments, their contingent of war vehicles and tanks, where they were moving. Things like that. The first physician to see him thought it was unusual for someone his age who had also been in a camp to have this information, and he called the

Army. He was then moved into the V.A. Hospital and he has been there ever since. I should tell you immigration officials were contacted also. They don't know the identity of this man. I don't trust their record-keeping anyway. Especially following the war, there was a lot of confusion."

"Is it my father?" Elie whispered.

"This man is very sick," the Doctor warned. "He's conscious for short periods, and then sleeps for days at a time. His heart affects his abilities. There's so little we know about this man. I . . . I . . ."

"The information he knew was not about the Nazis," Mrs. Arbiter continued scowling at the doctor. "It was about German positions during World War I. That's what he knew. That's all that he knew and that's what he went on about. There's more also. Nothing is definite, but there is more. Can I tell you the rest? Are you okay?"

"Yes."

"In his moments of consciousness he has spoken with the nurses there. Sometimes he is more lucid than at other times."

"Tell me the rest," Elie pleaded.

"Elie, do you understand that there is no certainty here. We can't say that this man is your father. We don't know for sure."

"What else do you know?"

"He claims," Mrs. Arbiter said, "to have worked for something called the *Abenpost*. And, he has not told anyone his name. The doctors don't think he can remember it, but some of the nurses — well some of the nurses think that he has called himself *Der Hebraisch Held*. They are not sure, Elie. Not very much makes sense, they've said, when he talks, but some think he calls himself that. One even wrote it down on her clipboard. She did not know what it meant and she was worried that he was complaining that he was in pain. She wrote the words down: *Der*

Hebraisch Held. It was a bit unusual. That's why one of the doctors remembered it."

"He came to look for us," Elie said. "We had already left. Mordechi was dead. He didn't know where to look. I should have looked for him there. I should have looked. I could have helped him."

"He's mouthing words in semi-consciousness," Doctor Chamberlain said. "And from this picture, I don't know. It's too old." He handed it back to Elie.

"We'd like you to go see this man," Avi Pilson said. "Can you do that? You should go. I don't think you're going to be disappointed."

Mrs. Arbiter pushed tickets to the edge of the desk. "Frana Luftwantz had the agency purchase a train ticket for you and your mother. I've written down all the information you'll need."

Elie felt tears dripping onto his sleeves and hands. "I don't know what to say or how to thank you."

A woman approached the desk.

"Elie, this is Frana Luftwantz. She runs the agency," Mrs. Arbiter said.

"I think, some help to you, we might have been," Frana said. She was small and slumped and her eyes were sunken deeply into her face. She shook Elie's hand, and touched his cheek. "Hopefully to your mother also." She took the frame from Elie and ran her hand along the glass.

"I'm so glad to meet you," Elie said, standing.

"Come, I'll walk you out."

Elie made his farewells and repeated his thanks and walked with Frana Luftwantz across the expanse of the warehouse.

"This agency, it used to be in the basement of Khal Anshei Chessed," she said. "Not so long ago."

"Rabbi Kishenev told me. I'm glad the city found you some extra space."

"The Congregation of Khal Anshei Chessed, they are good people. A bit old-fashioned perhaps, but their hearts are in the right place. The rebbe's son, Bernard Liebenshul, occasionally he helps here. Do you know him?"

"I've heard a lot about him." Elie knew she wanted to say more. "He's going to marry Dina Kishenev, I think."

She stopped, put a hand on his arm, squinting at him. "Do they love each other? When you talk to her, does she say these words? Are they in love?"

Elie wanted to reveal everything to this woman. She had helped him, and now he wanted to spill out the truth to her. He loved Dina, and she loved him. At another time and place, they would be together. Happy. If not for the circumstances Dina would've been there with him today. "Yes. Yes. She told me that she loves him."

"You lie poorly, but you at least your heart is in the right place."

Elie realized she was a congregant of Adas Yeraim. He knew he promised to protect Dina.

"No, I only went to see if she was okay after I hit her. Honest. She loves Bernard. She told me a hundred times. They are going to be married."

"You have many difficulties in your life right now. The most significant is about to take place when you speak to your mother in the next hour." She peered back at the agency offices. "You don't have to accept Rebbe Liebenshul's view of the world. The Holocaust is over. At least for now. Storm troopers are not likely to be seen on Dorchester Avenue any time soon. They are not coming for us, and Dina Liebenshul shouldn't sacrifice her life to soothe some old rebbe's fears. We all practice the faith in our own way. Merging the congregations will do nothing but ruin that poor child's happiness."

Elie wanted to hug her. He thought about his mother,

waiting for him, and about Naomi Moscow's message from Dina. He missed Dina. When he wasn't wondering about his father, she was all he could think about. "I think she's made up her mind," he said.

"Her mind," Frana said, "has been made up for her." She turned away. "Go tell your mother what you've found here. And good luck in Chicago."

"No," Lena Wasserman pleaded. "No, I cannot go. You should see this man, but I'll stay here." She rose and walked toward the kitchen.

It seemed almost impossible to Elie that the man in the photograph was still alive. The picture had always felt like a memorial to Elie; like an epitaph, helping Elie to remember him, even when his few actual memories dimmed. When he looked at the likeness, he had always felt his father was there, watching over him. How was it even imaginable that this sentinel had guarded him from a place closer than heaven?

Elie followed his mother to the kitchen. *What happened to you all these years ago?* Elie thought. *Is it too terrible to tell? Even to me?*

"Only one thing I am asking you to promise to me," Lena Wasserman said. "Bring him back to me. Promise me this . . . you will bring him back to us."

"I promise."

"Put your things into a suitcase. Then you can go."

Elie kissed his mother. "I promise you, I will bring him back. Don't worry anymore."

He went to gather his clothes, his heart nearly bursting with anticipation.

"Oh, and did you see the letter?"

Elie stopped. "What?"

"The letter, there for you on the table in the foyer."

"A letter? From who?"

Elie trembled. He knew it would be from Dina. His mother did not answer.

"I have it," Elie said. He turned the envelope over in his hands several times. He didn't want to hear anymore about how devoted Dina had decided to be to Bernard. He wondered whether he was destined to miss her throughout his entire life. It felt as if he would. I don't know if I can read this, he thought. He tore the envelope anyway.

Dear Elie,

I sat down tonight to write you this letter and I realized that you would probably throw it away without even reading it. I tried to think of reasons you might not, but I couldn't convince myself that I'd blame you if you did.

If you have thrown this away, and if I'm talking only to pieces of discarded paper and other crumpled letters, so be it. I need to say what I am now putting down on this paper, and even if you never read it, I think I'll feel better when I am finished for having taken the time to write down the way I am feeling. In any event, I feel a bit discarded tonight myself. Please understand, not by you. You always seem to be around just when I was thinking about you most or wanting so badly to talk to you before we had to stop being together. You were there when I looked up from something wondering where you might be or what you might be doing. It's the other people around me who seem, tonight, to be looking right by me even when I'm speaking to them. Sometimes I think I must be just a ghost or just an image in someone's imagination. Now that I've served my purpose and agreed to create a bridge for the congregations to cross and join together, it's almost as if I've disappeared. My usefulness has waned.

Please don't understand this in the wrong way. I love my family with all of my heart. As I've told you, I'd do anything and everything my father asked me to do to help him. His mission in life is so noble and worthy. My feelings, even my very life, pale in comparison, so I swear to you I'm not complaining about my lot.

Still, I need to tell you what follows here. And these items I tell you in confidence and pray that you will understand. First I want you to know that I am in awe of Bernard Liebenshul and that I respect him as I respect my father. He is brilliant and he is kind and gentle. He is someone who is more than entitled to my admiration and my devotion. Even with all of his wonderful traits however, I do not love Bernard Liebenshul. I could not love him as the truth is, I barely know him. When we're together he is engaged in discussion with my father. When we're alone, it's as if an ocean divides us though we are of a common water. We know our destinies and they are joined, but out of necessity and not enchantment.

To some, of course, this would be sad. Yet about this I am only resigned. Nevertheless, there is another matter that does make me sad. Tearful, actually, nearly mournful if you must know.

Elie, this thought that makes me sad, and the single thought of mine which I hope will linger with you long after this letter, is this paltry fact about me: I am in love with you. This is my fate and the one truth onto which I will hold forever. Please do not misunderstand what I am writing here. It's not my feelings for you that has brought me to my sadness. Instead, it is that I am bound inextricably to another and that nothing can sever those ties. The knots that bind me are tightened by the battle against persecution. They are ties that are not meant to be broken for they've been braided together with principle and righteousness. Nevertheless, in spite of the gleam of virtue shining from them, they weigh heavily on me.

Please also, as you read this, disregard my prior messages through Naomi. A feeble effort on my behalf to spare you from missing me. Why, in any event, I would think that anyone like you, kind and caring and so full of possibility, would miss the likes of me, I don't know. Self-delusion, probably. Wishful thinking perhaps. In any event, please forgive me. Before I go, and before you think ill of me (more ill of me), please one last thought; remember this: I'm not writing these words today so that you'll pity me and I'm, more than anything else, not writing to you so that you'll lament what might have been (if indeed you ever had such thoughts) had my future been free. I am writing to tell you to please have a beautiful life filled with all the happiness and wonder you can find. Somewhere, there is a beautiful girl whose path you will cross and who will treat you with kindness and a perfect smile. I can practically see her in my mind and feel her hand on your face. She is lovely and her devotion to you radiates from her. She knows all of the things about you that I do just from our brief moments together, and I need to tell you that, whoever she is, she is the most fortunate girl alive.

I must go now. I'm crying and my time for tears has passed. It's time for me to move on, to take on the tasks required of me. Before I close, however, I must ask two things of you. The first is a request and only that. It is selfish of me to even raise, but since just by the asking it will give me comfort as time rolls by, I will. Elie, some time in the future, when night has fallen, when you are alone watching a cloud pass over a full moon, when all is quiet and your beautiful wife and children are tucked away for the night, when you're resting on your porch after a day of writing, when your mind is filled with all of the joys life has in store for you, when you are by yourself, alone with your thoughts; please, just once, sometime, please, think of me. And remember me. You can be sure that I'll think of you often even as I stand by the side of Bernard Liebenshul. Sitting here today I can tell you without uncertainty that it will help me to know that it's possible, even perhaps just once, that you too have spent a moment recalling my odd face, the feel of our hands gripped together, and our last kisses on my doorstep.

For this small favor, I thank you in advance.

The second request is not a request at all. Instead, it is a promise that I must ask of you and it is a promise that you must pledge to keep forever without wavering.

If you ever had any feelings for me at all, no matter how insignificant, I implore you to help me with this one pact. Elie, if you are reading this, please promise me that you will never tell anyone about this letter or about what I have written on this paper. These thoughts, which I have put down are for you only, so that you will know forever how I feel. If my father were to hear of these things, it would break his heart. Entire congregations would be disappointed in me and angry with my parents. They don't deserve such a fate nor does Bernard Liebenshul deserve to be saddled with the knowledge that his wife dreams of someone else. Promise me, please, that you will tell no one. I must hold you to this until I have reached my grave. It is the one single thing, above all others, that I pray you will grant me.

And now I am finished. My sleeves are damp with tears and I am feeling tired, so I must end here. I will be asleep soon and I thank God for the rest. As for you, I thank you for knocking some passion into my life (the basketball was an abrupt start but perhaps that is what it took).

Elie, more than anything else, I hope you find your father and that he's alive and well. I will pray for that every day. I only hope that someday someone loves me and struggles for me as you do for your parents. They are both so lucky to have you.

Please remember always that thoughts of you consume me and also that

I love you,
Dina

Elie folded the letter, rubbed it with his fingers, and began to cry. He felt in his pocket for the ticket. There it was. A picture appeared in his imagination. It was of the man in the photograph driving a car, refugees hidden under his seat, his journalist's pass pressing into his hip from his jacket pocket. A single bead of sweat formed on his brow. The man, Elie suddenly knew, was contemplating the fate of his infant son, even as he pirated the innocent to safety. The son was far away, Elie could see. The man prayed to God to watch over his child.

MARCH 1992

When I arrived on the porch the following morning, Hersh was already there poking at the keyboard and mumbling in satisfaction. I considered asking him whether he had started drafting the final chapter, but such an inquiry might reveal that I had loitered near his room the previous night. To amuse myself, however, for the next several minutes I crafted coy questions in my head. Have you reached Hannah's saccharin ending yet? How many pages have you written? That kind of thing. I finally abandoned the idea altogether. The effort of talking to Hersh was not worth the embarrassment of his knowing that I cared. After all, I didn't care. I was just passing time.

Wanting tea, I looked for Belinda, but she was nowhere in sight. I decided to wait rather than to fetch the drink myself since that was her job, and I was too old and tired to get it without help anyway. Accordingly, I opened the book in my lap.

I did not care for *Tender is the Night* when I first read it, but since it's a classic, I thought I should try again. The blinds on the window behind me weren't drawn, but the slats had been opened, casting shadows across the room. There was certainly enough light to read, but as I was looking for excuses not to, I again looked around for Belinda to illuminate the overhead lamps or raise the shades. She was still absent, which was somewhat odd for that hour of the morning, but as I was sure she'd lumber in shortly, I shut my eyes to rest. Hersh ignored me.

Voices disturbed me from the foyer. There was a cadre of staff at the nurses' station and they sounded upset and frantic. I heard someone running. A gurney rolled by too fast. I glanced at Hersh, but he continued to poke at the keys.

The other residents began to arrive. Gertie Nuestadt walked in first and adjusted the lights. I granted her the briefest smile, but she ignored me.

Next to arrive, were the knitters, followed by the Swertlick brothers, all of whom appeared unfazed by any news. They began to argue about whose turn it was to control the television.

A few moments later, Harry wandered in with his entourage, and the room was immediately consumed by a tiff over who was responsible for his poker failures the previous day. I did my best to block out that discussion. I was convinced that if they had known of anything unexpected, they would not have been so predictable.

The other usual suspects filed in soon after that, Margolis, followed by Rose Goodman. Even Dr. Nathan made a brief appearance to absentmindedly greet everyone before returning to his walls. No one seemed aware of anything unusual, and I wondered if I'd heard anything at all, or if I had dozed off momentarily and dreamed the unrest I was now trying to verify. I waited for an orderly or Belinda, but no one came. Indeed, the only conduct that was at all uncommon was that Hersh, on the arrival of each resident, would glance up fleetingly over his monitor, watch the person, then look away. I wasn't sure whether anyone else noticed this scrutiny, but there was no question that he grew more anxious as the porch filled up.

Nearly an hour passed while this routine continued. Belinda still had not appeared, which was not remarkable, except that I was sure her voice was one I had heard in the hallway earlier. She was one of the few staff members who didn't loiter in the hallways or at the nurses' station, and this was good and bad since I hated her doting, but I could generally depend on her to help me when I wanted her to. The one time she decides to gossip is the exact day I need her, I complained to myself. I noticed Hersh glancing up again as a card player limped in. He was frowning when he returned to the monitor. Hannah Cohen had still not arrived.

Finally, I opened my book to the first page. I read the first sentence, then read it again, realizing I had not absorbed a single word. I looked up again at Hersh, who was tapping his watch. I wondered what he was thinking.

Finally, Belinda appeared at the doorway. Hersh and I both stared at her for a moment, but Hersh turned away. I was prepared to be belligerent, to let her know I didn't appreciate her ignoring her duties, but the words died before I said them. She seemed ravaged and aged, alone in a room full of people. Her hair, normally tied tightly in braids, was disheveled. Her smock, always bleached beyond whiteness, was stained and smeared.

Except for Hersh, everyone watched her. She had been crying, that much was clear, though it occurred to me that there was a difference between crying — the mere shedding of tears — and the outpouring of emotion, the intense weeping that was evident from her face, which was swollen red, and her eyes, which were puffy and bloodshot.

She shuffled along the floor almost dizzily as if her equilibrium had been damaged, and every few steps she'd stop and clutch a chair back. Before going on she would sigh and then look back longingly to the nurses' station. I could not see whether anyone was there, but I envisioned Brody standing at attention, the other staff members huddled around him, the entire group watching her as she went through this ordeal.

"Belinda?" someone said, softly.

She did not respond, but continued to struggle on her way. When she reached Mrs. Silver's chair, she paused again.

Their faces were remarkably similar; agony sketched on each, and, as I focused, I was stunned by their mutual pain. Mrs. Silver's was physical, I knew, almost identical to Sarah's, near the end, and Belinda's was more intangible — heartbroken, devastated. But the intensity of their misery was inescapable, and I understood, then, that for Belinda to feel such grief there could be only one cause.

She reached out and placed her palm gently upon Mrs. Silver's cheek. There was an expression of longing on Mrs. Silver's face, but I guessed even that did not reveal the helplessness the poor woman felt at that moment. "God has made an error," she whispered almost inaudibly. "I've been prepared for a long time."

A minute went by while they held each other's hands. Finally, Belinda shivered. She drew a chair up next to Hersh and sat.

Hersh began to shake his head, rapidly at first and then in long agonized denial. Belinda tried to wrap her arm around his shoulder, but he pushed her away.

She waited for a moment while he waved his arms at the air in front of him. Then they fell onto each other and held one another's grief.

My throat clogged with dryness and I swallowed to clear it. My eyes welled too, though I fought back the emotion with all the willpower I could muster. I did not know, then, whether I was mourning for Hannah Cohen or Sarah or myself. Whatever, my own feelings didn't matter. Hersh was the one who now, too, would be forced to live with loneliness.

Ten minutes passed, and they did not move. The stillness between them was heart wrenching, and some of those around them wept and seemed to wither, too.

Finally, Hersh rose. Belinda stood also and whispered something to him that I could not hear. In one motion, Hersh switched off the computer, gathered the discs and papers from the table, and moved toward the door. Halfway there, however, he stopped. "Did I leave anything?" he asked.

Belinda shook her head, stood up and peered around the porch.

"I am so sorry." Belinda's expression of helplessness had not changed.

"It's all right, Belinda," Margolis said. "You don't have to say anything."

"Well, I do want you to know there was no pain. I'm sorry."

Belinda was crying as she wobbled to the door.

My reaction to Hannah Cohen's death, at least after the initial shock of it, was measured indifference. Yes, she was a pleasant enough woman, and indeed she had certain qualities that were reminiscent of Sarah, but I was too old, too tired, and too drained of feelings to dwell on this death as if it were personal. There would be no long-term effect on me as a result of her passing, I knew. And I was convinced her time had simply come, so there was no need to think she had died prematurely or unnecessarily. Besides, there was a distinct possibility that where she was now was much preferable to remaining ensconced at Emunah.

This view was not shared by the others. Over the next weeks the porch was little more than a mourning parlor. The residents who came and went appeared locked in a funeral procession, their eyes were cast downward, their gaits a step more heavy. No one stayed long on the porch, either. It was just too painful to be near to where Hannah Cohen used to sit.

In deference to her memory, there were no card games played and no jokes told during the week of her Shiva or for several weeks after. There were, also, no loud demands made of Belinda, or any complaints made to any of the staff. Gertie and her cohorts continued their sewing and knitting, and many people continued to read, but everyone's conversation dwindled, and even the television was kept off for an extended time, its ubiquitous noise seeming inappropriate, even to those addicted to it.

While, I did not expend much energy on grieving, Hannah Cohen's death did inspire its own brand of moroseness. I began to have nightmares again, and inescapable daydreams as well. I remembered Sarah's agony while she lay in the hospital. Her fear of dying, though she was brave, came back to me in vivid images of glazed eyes and lips and skin cracked dry with fever. She was frail, no, emaciated, and the pale of her face was an apparition in my subconscious. "Please let me help you," I would call out, trembling in my sleep. But I would awaken in my room, my thoughts awash in shame and guilt and misery.

I didn't go to the service for Hannah Cohen. Hersh didn't either, but there was a dispute about whether his absence was due to tradition not being properly observed — no rabbi could be located, thus, the funeral was delayed several days — or whether he was simply too ill with grief to attend. People do extraordinary things while they are mourning, so his failure to attend the ceremony was not all that surprising.

Yet, there was much discussion of Hersh's absence from the service in the days after Hannah Cohen's burial. Allegations of insensitivity and lack of common courtesy were the main topics, and *gonif* and *mumzer* were two words I heard frequently.

I took no part in these conversations. Hersh was entitled to be shaken, and he did nothing to merit the verbal lashings he was enduring. Moreover, he had lost not only his companion, but his mentor as well, leaving him in a precarious state. I was certain that the book project, which had been the centerpiece of his life, along with Hannah Cohen, for the past months, now would simply die. There was no way the poor wretch could continue on his own. He had neither the technical knowledge nor the ability to persevere.

Hersh, for his part, did not defend himself either; he simply did not return to the porch. I looked for him each morning, as I always had, but his seat was vacant when I arrived, so I would cross to my spot, professing that I was delighted for the quiet and the calm. He did not appear at meals, or in the halls either, and no one spoke of seeing him in the weeks that followed. As the time passed, we heard less and less of him from the staff.

Eventually, the harping by the residents gave way to longing. "Life continues," Rose moaned one afternoon. "People die, life continues — enough already. He should come back to us."

I agreed with Rose in principle, but not because we had anything to continue toward, but simply because I myself grew exasperated at his absence. I was so annoyed, one evening, I wheeled to his room, to beg him to make a simple appearance; anything in order to curtail the mostly toothless mob that dwelled on his errors in protocol.

What I found, however, was a room so hushed and still that it appeared condemned. The door was shut and locked, and though I thought about knocking, I heard nothing inside and decided against such intrusion. I listened, with my ear nearly touching the door, but there was no movement, no sound, not even a creaking bed. Was he even there? I did not know, and I wheeled away, telling myself that I did not care.

Rumors of Hersh's whereabouts started after a time, and though it brought no comfort, it at least provided variety. One piece of gossip had him on his deathbed in the convalescent wing. Another had him as Emunah's first suicide (the scuttlebutt was that he had been found with a dagger plunged into his chest the morning after Hannah's passing). Predictably, Maury was certain once again, that Hersh had escaped, and actually looked gratified that he might be right. As no one could dispute him, I believe this became the rumor of choice.

I had no idea where Hersh had sequestered himself, though I was quite certain he was neither ill, nor dead, nor wandering the countryside looking for safe haven. Instead, I believed he was ignoring us purposely, fighting with himself to rekindle the energies he had first displayed.

It'll be difficult for him, I thought. He was aging, and renewal at his stage of life was unlikely, especially in the face of such tragedy.

I was surprised one morning, to find that the computer had been removed, appropriated in the dead of night. This might create upheaval among the residents, I thought. They often interpreted change as a personal affront. Harry might object to his gift being carted away, or Belinda might question this act as surrender.

But no one even noticed it was missing. Had Hersh taken the machine? Was he working? That was doubtful. But who then, and for what purpose? I was struck by the indignity that it had just been taken away; that someone had decided that we had no use for it, and an administrative decision had been made to remove it. Put it in storage, they will break it if we leave it there, let's get it out of harm's way, I heard Brody saying in my imagination. I looked around and knew with certainty why I felt unnerved. The porch, or perhaps more appropriately the residents, had been recast back to the roles we had played prior to Hersh's arrival. It was as if a magnet had drawn us back, or as if we were settled back by the force of gravity. There were readers, and card players, and those who watched TV. There were those who knit, and staff members and orderlies and myself sitting off to the side, exiled by choice. They were right to remove the machine, I realized. We had absolutely no use for it now that Hersh and Hannah were gone. We were not even entitled to keep it as an icon; there were no more symbols of hope on the porch.

I looked down at the book in my lap: *Ragtime,* and for as long as a week I read voraciously. I was so spellbound with the novel, and so completely detached from the events taking place around me, that I failed to notice when Hersh caned his way inside, and pushed his way with tiny shuffle steps to the edge of my chair. What alerted me was Belinda calling to him from the doorway. "Sam — Sam — Are you all right?"

My first thought was nonsensical; relief that Maury was once again proved to be a fool. Hersh obviously had not escaped. When I realized that he was standing over my chair, staring at me with eyes that were difficult to avert, Maury vanished from my thoughts.

He was dressed, as always, in his suit, but the clothes now seemed to dangle on him and billow aimlessly. His face, too, seemed more than just thinned. His cheeks and eyes were gaunt, and there were patches of bloodless blue on his forehead and chin.

I wanted to turn away. Agony and heartsickness were unmistakable in his decimated features. I would have given anything for him to go away at that moment or for Belinda to wrap her arm around his shoulder and guide him gently from the room. His anguish was nearly unbearable to witness.

"Sam? What is it?" I said.

He shifted slightly under his clothes almost as though he was uncomfortable with their weight. I noticed, only then, from his awkward stance, that he clutched a pile of paper to his side with one arm. As my eyes shifted, he rested his cane against a chair, took the pile into both hands and seemed to gauge its heaviness by rocking it back and forth before caressing the top sheet with his thumbs. I could see the trepidation in his face.

"Sam?"

"I finished it myself," he muttered. "The last chapter, I did it alone after Hannah — after she passed away"

"Okay," I responded. My heart was pounding but I did not know whether I was unnerved or just wildly confused.

He placed the papers gently on my lap. "You were right," he whispered. "All this time, the way you think, you — you were right."

"What do you mean?"

He ignored me and walked away. Belinda finally came to his aid.

I had no idea why Hersh had chosen me to be his proofreader; perhaps, I thought, it was my background or perhaps he imagined I would have the least jaundiced eye. In any case, I considered relinquishing the manuscript.

I placed my book on the floor and ran my thumb up the corner of the stack to measure the task that lay ahead. I felt genuine dread. Reading it appeared to be my obligation. And, what would be expected of me afterward? I would have to fawn over the effort they had made, and view the work in the most positive light. One of the authors was dead, and the other desperately needed encouragement. How could I criticize such a thing, even if it was horrible?

I glanced down at the top page and read the single word typed there in bold capital letters: UNTITLED. The others patients were staring back at me. And unpalatable, I thought. Sarah would read Hersh and Hannah's work joyfully. Sarah is dead I answered, nearly out loud.

"Oye," I whispered, shaking my head. I picked up the stack and started to read.

MAY 1948

By
Sam Hersh

A man spit on Elie's shoes as he walked. He was an older man. A dying man, there in the hospital. He was on a stretcher near the door. His eyes were shut but only halfway. His face was stubbled and his beard was spotted with blood and dirt. To Elie, he smelled of whiskey.

Elie moved by and looked to see if a nurse was near. Anyone to help the man. No one seemed available. There were many others there also waiting for help.

Around the screens, behind the DOCTORS ONLY sign, Elie heard another man yelling. It was a wail actually. The voice trailed off into sobbing and a plea to heaven to take him. "Shut him up," Elie heard a younger voice order. Elie guessed it was a doctor. "It is hard enough in here without that garbage."

Elie moved down the corridor and looked for an open room where he could ask someone where to go. He looked for an office or a sign to direct him. He frowned at the smell, which was neither exactly like urine nor vomit, but a mixture of the two.

The hallway was dim.

"What do you want?" the woman behind the desk demanded, when Elie stepped inside the door marked RECORDS. "What are you doing here?"

"I'm looking for Dr. Chamberlain." He hesitated. "He told me to meet him here."

"In records? In this office? This is where he told you to meet him? You have made a mistake. No one meets here. Go to the main office."

"He told me to meet him at the hospital. Not here. I didn't mean to disturb you."

"The main office or the fourth floor. Convalescence. I think that's his department. Visitors should not be in this corridor. Don't come back if you can't find him. Go to the admissions desk. They should help you, not me."

"Convalescence?"

"If you go up there, be quiet. There are many men there still recovering. Very sick men. Most will probably never go home. That is their home. So be quiet."

Elie returned to the hall and retraced his steps until he came to the door marked STAIRS.

Going up, Elie listened to the sounds that echoed through the walls. Terrible groans and cries for help came from everywhere. There was activity, too, voices yelling commands and footsteps running back and forth.

On the third-floor landing, a man lay sleeping. His hospital gown was untied and barely covered him. Elie knelt over him, but the patient did not move. This was a younger man, younger at least than the man Elie saw when he first arrived. He had no visible scars or wounds either. Elie wondered why he was there.

"Excuse me," Elie called out to a nurse across the hall, after opening the door and holding it open with his foot. "Excuse me, there is a man here. He does not seem to be moving and I don't think he is where he should be." The nurse did not move.

Elie continued to climb. He opened the door on the forth level and before him was one large room covering the entire floor. It was not as decrepit and filthy as what he had seen before. Nevertheless, this only distracted him from the tragedy that appeared before his eyes. Rows of beds stretched off into the distance, none more than two feet from the next or more than a yard from those in the adjacent rows. Between each bed was a table and a lamp, nothing more, and each bed was the same, a cot with ivory-colored blankets. As far as Elie looked, he could not see a single empty mattress.

What seemed to him like ten thousand eyes followed him. As he walked down what appeared to be the center aisle, the stares went with him.

Everywhere there were men, bandaged and broken. Dazed men with legs or arms missing and cotton gauze wrapped where their limbs should have been. Men with holes so deep in their chests or their skulls, Elie wondered how they could possibly be alive.

He tried not to stare. One could not be in this room without being struck by the terrible suffering and lonely despair. There were several other visitors there, parents mostly, it appeared.

"Can I help you?" It was a nurse, several rows down, who made the inquiry. She was attending to a patient who clung to her sleeve. She shook off the man's hand. "Can I help you?" she asked again, this time with annoyance.

"I'm looking for Dr. Chamberlain. I am supposed to see him about — about a man that may be in the hospital, here."

"He's gone. He went home. He's not here."

"I was supposed to find him when I arrived. I . . . I . . . thought —"

"He's not here, I said."

Elie did not know what to do. He turned around and walked back toward the stairs.

"What patient are you here to see?" The nurse called to him. "Who is it?" She was moving around beds toward him.

"Look, there are a lot of patients here," she said, "I can't waste a lot of time. Who are you looking for?"

"I . . . I don't know what name he is here under," Elie admitted, realizing he had not asked anyone. "*Der Hebraisch Held* is all I know."

"Oh, that's you, huh," the nurse said. "This way." He followed her. "What are you, from the army or something? You don't look like you are."

"I think he's my father," Elie whispered.

The nurse looked at Elie. Elie felt in his pocket for the picture he had been told to bring. It was there. "I don't think so," the nurse muttered. "I could be wrong, but I don't think so."

Elie did not know what to say. He was breathing hard and trying to remember what he had promised himself he would say when he saw his father.

"You can ask him, I guess," the nurse said. "He is more coherent now. Not great, but better. He might understand you." They walked farther. "Around here."

They reached a canvas divider. "Around there," the nurse said. "Being around the others made him nervous. And loud. All sorts of ranting." She frowned at Elie. "Go ahead."

Elie was out of breath. He thought about his mother and Menachem Kultz before he moved. "It has been so long," he whispered to himself, "I hope I know him."

He circled the divider and finally, after a moment of looking away, Elie turned to the bed before him. He bent to the man there and studied his face. He removed the picture from his pocket and gazed at it. His eyes went from the soldier in the tintype to the frail man lying, unaware of him, on his side in the bed. He was huddled, squeezing his knees. The man in the picture was tall, and broad. His features were square and strong. The man in the bed was small and frightened. His eyes drooped and his mouth hung open as if he was too tired even to press his lips together. Elie continued to look and compare. These were not the same faces. He knew immediately: This man was not his father.

The nurse was suddenly behind him, inspecting the picture over his shoulder. On her lips was a sneer. "I didn't think so," she confirmed, shaking her head. "That's not him. I could tell just from the chin. You have different chins. That is always how I know." She shrugged. "Too bad."

In the bed, the man began to stir.

"Can you find your way back to the stairs?"

"This is the man who calls himself *Der Hebraisch Held*?" Elie asked. "There must be a mistake."

The nurse looked annoyed. "This is him. It's on his papers. He uses those words. I don't know if he calls himself that or if he just uses those words but this is the man." Elie knew she was angry. "Do you want to stay or do you want help finding the stairs?"

Elie stepped to the side of the bed and stared at the patient's face. The man's eyes were wide open now and he gazed off into the distance, out the small window a few feet away. Elie sat on the edge of the mattress. "I'm going to sit a minute. I'll find my own way out."

"Don't upset this patient. You have no right to agitate him."

"It's okay," Elie confided to the man who continued to look away. Elie did not know what else to say. He had no idea even what language the man spoke or whether he could hear anything at all. He paused and thought. "*Der*

Hebraisch Held," Elie finally whispered. "I'm the son of *Der Hebraisch Held.*"

The patient seemed startled, and he shuddered and tried to move away. His face became filled with suspicion. For a long period he studied Elie. "The Gestapo. Now, they have come for me?"

"No," Elie assured him. "No. No. You're safe here," Elie assured the man. "This is a hospital. In the United States. You're safe here."

In the man's eyes there was still fear. *"Der Hebraisch Held."* He glared at Elie. He studied his face in careful detail. *"Der Hebraisch Held."* He raised his hands as if to protect himself and he tried with desperation to push his body farther away from Elie. "It is not possible. He is dead. They promised me in the camp that he was dead."

"No," Elie told the man. "My father. He was *Der Hebraisch Held.*" The man listened but Elie could not tell if he understood. "Did he help you escape? *Der Hebraisch Held,* he helped you get out of Germany? Or your family, did they escape?"

"My beautiful family — they are dead," the man shouted. His eyes were wide with anger. "Dead." His face twisted into sadness. "They are dead," he uttered, his voice barely able to be heard. "My Meir, and my Chana — and my little Lily — My Lily," he began to hum. "My little Lilytonka," he sang, "my Lilytonka." Onto the pillow, a tear fell from his cheek. Such sadness came over the man, Elie thought that it might be possible that he could die from such heartbreak alone.

"What is your name?" Elie asked softly. "Can you tell me that? What is your name?"

The patient did not respond. He rocked his head on his pillow and continued to hum. Elie was certain this was a lullaby of some kind from earlier and happier days. The man pulled his knees back up to his chest.

"Do you have a name?" Elie said, not expecting an answer.

With his fingers wrapped weakly around Elie's sleeve, the man pulled himself up. His eyes moved around the room as if he was waiting for someone to take him away. His hands trembled. "*Der Hebraisch Held,* he will send them to look," he whispered. "They will come here. He will send them."

"Who will he send?" Elie asked. "What are you talking about?"

"Go to safety." The man pushed Elie's shoulder. "Go."

"Who will he send?" Elie said again. "*Der Hebraisch Held* is going to send someone to you?"

"The Gestapo, the SS, they will come when he asks."

Elie was confused. "He'll take you to safety. *Der Hebraisch Held.* Into Switzerland. Away from danger. Away from the Gestapo."

"No. No. Do not go with him," the man begged. "Do not have trust in this man. No."

"He will help you," Elie urged.

"Do not trust him," the man warned, "you will die. Your family will die. So many Jews trusted him. Now they are in graves. Do not go with him."

"You're wrong. You are talking about someone else," Elie protested. He pulled the man's hand from his sleeve and stood up. "You're confused."

The man's hands fell to his sides. Elie could see that his arms were little more than bones covered with loose, gray skin. On his forearm, a number had been branded by the Germans.

"It's someone else," Elie declared.

He listened as the man mumbled prayers and shut his eyes. He said the Kaddish and called out names.

Elie was dizzy. "Emil Wasserman? Was that the man? Was that the man you're talking about? *Der Hebraisch*

Held?" He leaned down to the patient. "My father did not do the things you have said. It's not possible."

"A Jewish man — You too are a Jew," the man cried. "Why would you do this to your own people?"

"These are lies," Elie begged. "Why are you saying these things?"

"That will be enough," the nurse ordered. "You're disturbing everyone."

"He drove people to Switzerland," Elie whispered to himself, "with his journalist's pass. He helped them escape."

"Have you joined the Jewish Police? Is that what you are? The Jewish Police?" the man asked. He stared ahead as if he could see the man he was speaking to.

Elie knew that Jewish Police referred to those Jews in the Warsaw Ghetto in Poland who, in exchange for better food and living arrangements, informed on those Jews in the Resistance and on others who did not follow the rules of the Nazi regime. Most who were informed on were murdered.

The nurse moved closer to them. "Everyone has to leave now. The time for visiting is over."

"No . . . No, you are a soldier. You are fighting for your Germany, your homeland, the Fatherland. You betray your own people for the Fatherland? This is what you do to us? *Der Hebraisch Held*."

"Your family?" Elie asked.

"Under the seat, my little Lily. And then Meir and Chana. They will not be able to breathe. The secret door. They will not be able to breathe so close together there," the man called out, as if still watching his children. "To Liestal. Over the border. Go. Go." His breathing grew short and he began to shiver. He grabbed Elie's sleeve. "To Majdanek he took them." He was barely able to speak. "So alone and frightened, my children. Into the hands of a madman, I put them."

"Is this the man?" Elie asked, holding the tintype near to the patient's eyes.

"No," the nurse said, pushing Elie's hand aside. "Enough for one day. This patient has had enough. Go. Enough is enough."

"So much fighting from the First War," the man mumbled to himself. "Such loyalty to Germany, from fighting in the First War. Seeing such terrible things then. Things done to young German soldiers so many years ago, so many years earlier. Horrible things. Terrible things. A madman he became — My children in the hands of a madman."

"Enough of this now. That is enough," the nurse said. Elie was on the other side of the divider. "Enough."

For a moment, as Elie listened, the patient hummed his lullaby again.

Elie turned away. He shuddered as he walked to the stairs.

Outside Adas Yeraim, Elie sat on the steps.

The trip home had been long. Elie had not slept for what, to him, seemed like days. When weariness had come to him on the train, he was always startled back awake by the words of the man in the hospital.

More than anything else, Elie wanted to speak to Dina. He wanted her to tell him that she loved him. That she loved him no matter what his father had done. He wondered how he could even tell her what he had learned. She was committed to marrying Bernard; to do what was necessary — even if it meant the sacrifice of her own dreams and happiness. And what could Elie say? He was, after all, it seemed, part of the plague. Somewhere inside him ran the blood of betrayal. How could he even look at her?

And what could he possibly tell his mother? Perhaps simply that her husband was dead, he thought. Perhaps a lie: It was someone else that the patient described, or that the patient had lost consciousness just as he arrived.

Elie wiped his forehead on his sleeve. He needed to tell Dina that he loved her. He needed to be with her. He realized that his life had changed and that she was a part of him. He wanted to tell her before it was too late, that he needed her; that he felt lost when they were apart. Confused. Frightened. Alone. The prospect that they would not be together again was inconceivable. He suddenly could not understand it. To him, it seemed like a thousand-pound weight on his shoulders. And this weight, it pressed on his lungs and made his breathing heavy and labored. "Dina, please," he whispered to himself, "I need you. I don't know how to be without you. Please. Help me."

He walked to the door around the corner and knocked. Softly, at first, and then louder, with his knuckles. Dina was close by. He could feel her there. The door opened. It was Mrs. Kishenev.

"Elie. Why have you come here now?" She stepped outside and shut the door behind her. "You can't come here. Dina can't see you. It's too late."

"Mrs. Kishenev, I need to tell her one thing. Just two minutes."

"Tell me and I will tell her. Is it about your father? Have you found him?"

Elie took a deep breath. "No," he murmured. "The man in the hospital was confused. It wasn't my father." He looked away.

"I'm sorry. I will ask the rebbe to say a prayer for you, and for your father. I promise I'll do that."

"Please," Elie asked again, "just for a moment."

Dina's mother frowned. After a moment of uncertainty, she nodded her assent. She turned and put her hand on the doorknob, then stopped, and stood motionless. "No. No," she shook her head. "No." She looked back at Elie. "No, you can't see her. My husband and I, we have decided. This is best for her. Bernard Liebenshul will be a good husband. This will help everyone. It's for the community. It's too important. This sacrifice I am willing to make of my daughter. Do you understand?"

Elie did not answer. He could not ask anything further. Exhaustion swept over him.

On the steps of Hecht House, Elie sat and listened as boys inside shouted and played. His mother would be home soon and he would tell her the truth. He would tell her all that the patient had told him. Everything — word for word.

He was tired. Weary. His body felt almost as if it was part of the step, the cement there, still. He felt empty. All the fervor had passed. All the good had departed. All hope was lost.

For a moment Elie could not remember how he came to be there on the steps at Hecht House. He tried to recall walking there, but no memory came to him. His body ached, but it was a dull pain, nothing to bandage and nothing that medicine could cure.

"I'm seventeen years old," he thought to himself. Tears filled his eyes. "And I think that I'm dead already." Slumped there, he wept until dark.

MAY 1992

I pressed the last sheet on top of the others that preceded it, and leaned back in my chair. My throat was dry and my arms felt weak. My face must have been ashen.

My neighbors waited for my reaction. Rose seemed prepared to ask what I thought, though she was reticent. Harry, from the poker table, peeked above his cards suspiciously, poised, it appeared, to unleash a tirade of criticism if I did not share my perceptions with him first. Belinda, too, threw furtive glances in my direction as she tended to Maury. She wore an expression of troubled anticipation, almost, I thought, as if she had guessed the dispiriting contortions wrought by Hersh in the story's conclusion.

I didn't know whether I was ready to reveal the dark details of what I had just read. They were certainly going to be disappointed, heartbroken — all of them — of that I was sure. But there was more that troubled me. It made no difference whether they had participated, I realized. This manuscript had been the center of their collective attention. Yes, they had declined to give the authors help. Nevertheless, for some time, not a day had passed in which the porch was not alive with excitement over the project. Once Hersh and Hannah had begun outlining, little else seemed to matter.

How will they react? I worried. Will they blame me? After all, Hersh's last words on the porch were directed to me. "You were right — You were right."

My thoughts circled backwards. I thought of Sarah in the hospital, weakened and resigned. I thought of my own fall down the stairs and of Dr. Glick and Jennifer Kent. Rose's painting of Abraham about to slay his son, next flashed in my mind, as, with a certain symmetry, did Hersh's words uttered through Mrs. Kishenev in the story: "This sacrifice I am willing to make of my daughter."

I had a vision of Hannah Cohen, mesmerized and enchanted, the day she came upon the story line that she and Hersh composed. There was a quality of sheer beauty about her I had not recognized when I saw her that day. That morning she had been magical in her hopefulness and her triumph, irresistible in her joy and her love of life. How could I not have been swept up in her enthusiasm, then? In her face, unmasked to me now — or perhaps more aptly put, more focused now in my eyes — was revelation, epiphany. It was as if God had touched her, given her a gift.

"Belinda," I called.

"Yes, Abe? What do you need?"

"I know you're busy," I said quietly, "but I need some paper. Do you think they have any behind the desk?"

"Are you finished?" she asked. She pointed to the stack of papers on the table next to me, then registered my urgency. "I'll get it for you."

"Thank you."

Sarah's face had a quality similar to that of Hannah Cohen's. The image I recalled was one from that afternoon many years earlier, on the day when she declared that she would become a teacher. How beautiful she was and full of life. There simply were no hardships, no disappointments. She had been inspired that day, exactly as I recalled Hannah Cohen.

"Is this enough, Abe?" Belinda placed a half dozen sheets on the table. "I brought a pencil too. I didn't know whether you had one or not."

"More than enough. And I did not have a pencil. Thank you. Good thinking."

Along with Sarah's lovely awakening, a series of other memories I thought I had long since lost flooded back to me.

I turned my chair to face the table, picked up the pencil, and tapped the eraser on the wood before flipping the point to my fingertips. I mulled my thoughts for perhaps a minute and then smoothed the paper in front of me.

I knew what I had to do.

AUGUST 1963
FIFTEEN YEARS LATER

By
Abe Gilman
(For Sam Hersh and Hannah Cohen)

Elie listened as the crickets began to call after dusk. Standing at the porch balustrade with the evening unfolding before him, the rush of the day seemed far off.

He thought of nothing for a while and the freedom from deliberation soothed him. He was not troubled, in fact he was at ease and relaxed. Nevertheless, the tranquility before him, the prevailing calm that made itself so plain from this perch, called for him to take stock.

He loosened his tie as the final flame of the sun turned gray. Stars were beginning to form in the distance, igniting into white points. He sat down in the lounge chair and wondered why he did not witness the night more often.

"Why are you out here in the dark, Dad?" Rachel asked, tiptoeing around the doorway and spotting her father. She was in her pajamas. Elie knew she had not put on socks.

"Your feet are going to get cold," Elie warned her. "Sit over here for a minute."

"No tickling," she commanded.

"No tickling."

Rachel sat on his lap and kissed his cheek. "Do you always sit out here in the dark? If you do, I'm going to tell Mom."

She had developed inflections in her voice already that mirrored her mother's; Elie was amazed at the similarities in tone and delivery. They had the same brown hair and opaque green eyes, but Elie did not see his wife in Rachel's features. The child was beautiful, as was Ellen, but to Elie their faces were distinct.

It's quiet out here," he said. "I like it."

"Dad —" she said, about to ask a question. She pressed her back against his chest.

"Rachel," her mother called, interrupting her, "can you help Josh clean up his room?"

"I didn't mess it up," she shouted back. "Okay. Okay. See ya." She waved and disappeared into the house.

Elie watched a cloud pass beneath the stars. He was lucky, he knew, perhaps more than he had a right to be. His parents had led difficult lives, as did many other people he had met over the years. And the earth was still filled with suffering, even after the Holocaust and even after the years following World War II. Yes, Elie was lucky to have met Ellen on the train from New York many years earlier, lucky to have healthy children, lucky to be able to live a peaceful life.

Ellen loved him. And he was, almost beyond reason, mesmerized by her and always had been.

He had the job he had yearned for. How many other journalists had the good fortune to be able to decide each day how to fill their columns with their own perceptions and ideas?

Rachel and Josh were talking just inside the door.

He was indeed fortunate.

His thoughts turned to his father and the time before he had finally proven that the war criminal described by the patient in the veteran's hospital was not he. After months of work and hundreds of hours spent drafting correspondence (to the military, to camp survivors, and to officials in Israel), Elie confirmed that the patient's betrayer was a man who came from Tübingen, not Freiburg, was neither Jewish nor a journalist, and was eventually killed by the Gestapo for alleged collaboration with the Russians near the end of the war.

This man had, in fact, fought for Germany during the First World War, Elie had discovered, and there was an unsubstantiated story — recited by the venerable Town Clerk in Tübingen — of him defending the doorway to a synagogue in Schaerbeek, Belgium, during an early counterattack by General Pétain in 1915. Hence, the clerk had surmised, the duplicated moniker, *Der Hebraisch Held*. Little, however, was available about the incident, and Elie realized this terrible man was simply expert at engaging the unwary and proficient at lying to gain their trust. He came to suspect that the incident at Schaerbeek had been fabricated, and that the man may have simply learned of his father and employed the nickname in a plot to send Jews to their deaths.

Of his actual father, Elie had also learned much. After the final Nuremberg trial, when thousands of documents were made public, Elie discovered that he had died at Dachau. He had been an advocate for many of the other prisoners there, Elie learned from accounts drafted by other prisoners. As one of the stronger men, he had been kept alive to work during his incarceration, and had stood up to his captors in defiance on numerous occasions. Eventually, he was shot, protesting the hanging of several boys accused of stealing. Seven years after his death, a rabbi said the Kaddish for him and his memory was laid to rest. Elie reflected on him often and with great pride.

Elie thought of his mother, then, and he remembered her stoic response when told of her of her husband's fate. She did not shed a tear nor did she grieve until the rabbi said the blessing for him. Then the period of the Shiva came and it seemed to Elie that she found relief. Two years later, she married Irwin Zelton, her employer, who had been widowed several months earlier. He retired after that and they had talked about moving, but Elie knew that leaving Josh and Rachel behind would be nearly impossible. She was still nearby.

"Can I listen to the Red Sox game? On my transistor radio?" Josh asked, coming around the corner. "In my bed?"

"You can if you give me a hug first."

Josh kissed his father, then squeezed him around the neck. "Are you okay, Dad? Mom says you're thinking. Seems boring. Earl Wilson's pitching. I'll use the little ear thing. I won't bother Rachel."

Elie watched his son run back into the house. "We already did our homework anyway," Josh called back.

Elie rested his head on the chair cushion. The years had whistled by, he thought. His recollections turned to Mattapan Square and the Hecht House gym and he wondered whether Hy was still alive. He remembered the apartment on Crossman Street, Yudie Kosasky, Menachem Kultz, and Gurlock's Hardware Store.

Without warning, the meandering over his past halted. His mind was immersed with memories of Dina Kishenev. Though he stared at the night, her face appeared before him. He had heard nothing of her in years, and yet it was almost as if she was close by; as if when he turned around she would be waiting, the look of hopefulness and the kindness he remembered, still illuminating her face.

She had married Bernard Liebenshul soon after Elie last visited the house. That much he remembered, as well as how sad he had been. His world had seemed empty until Ellen filled it.

He remembered the night he launched the fateful final shot against the team from St. Brigid's. In his mind, the gym was silent as the ball sailed through its arc and descended upon her. It seemed as if all else on earth had frozen in time when the ball left his hand. Only he and Dina Kishenev were there.

A hawk floated by the moon and Elie watched it glide until it disappeared into the gray, but Dina's face stayed with him. He remembered the way his heart beat when he saw her and the feeling of joy at her nearness. He remembered her encouragement as he searched for his father, unfolding the mysteries of his past and his heritage. And he remembered her kiss and the taste of her tears the night he last saw her.

Another image filtered into his imagination. Dina was sitting on the corner of her young son's bed stroking his hair and his cheek.

Where could she possibly be; where was this taking place? Somewhere out in this night, somewhere beyond the edge of his vision, somewhere in this same air he breathed, she was there.

At that precise moment she, too, thought of him, he knew. He could feel her out beyond the night.

He closed his eyes and thanked God for his memories. Good night, he bid her. The hush of his voice carried out into the darkness and beyond the night.

"What are you thinking about?" Ellen was at his side and there was worry on her face.

Elie's eyes were damp and a tear fell down his cheek. "I love you," he said. "That's all."

MAY 1992

I put down my pencil, and blinked at the sheets on the table before me. The pages were strewn about in a haphazard fashion. Almost by reflex, I gathered them together and organized my work.

The sensation I felt was as if I had been awakened, as if for the previous hours I had been elsewhere, far away, transported. I expected everyone would be staring at me, justifiably wondering whether I was completely mad.

No one was watching me. No one else was there.

I studied the room again to confirm that I had been somehow left behind. It was night. The blinds had been pulled. At the edges and beyond there was darkness.

I was confused and I turned back to the door to check the clock above the frame. Though the hands read 10:30, I was quite certain this was impossible. I had, after all, begun only minutes earlier. The product of my efforts, I had surmised, had come quickly, and, I had thought, without time-consuming edits or even minor revisions.

I examined the pages in my hands. Each sheet, I realized, was covered with miscues, and with arrows guiding circled phrases to some other point of more appropriate placement. The words had not flown easily. My task, though completed, had apparently come with a single-mindedness of purpose.

"Abe?" It was Belinda.

I gathered myself. "Belinda," I replied, "it's nearly eleven o'clock, dear. What are you still doing here?"

I knew, without question, that she had waited for me. "We were worried. You haven't moved for hours. And you missed dinner." Her expression was angelic. "You've been so busy. I was wondering if you needed anything? Is everything okay? Can I get you anything?"

My former attitude toward this woman returned to me, this time in waves of shame. She was good-hearted, yet I'd treated her with disdain, dismissing her good intentions as pretense and commonplace.

"I think everything'll be all right," I answered. "But I could use your help."

She approached. "I didn't want to interfere."

"Were you waiting here for me to finish?"

"I didn't know what was happening." She pointed to the stack of pages. "Is there something wrong with it? You looked troubled when you were done reading."

"It's so late," I suggested. "You must be exhausted. You came early this morning."

"Is there something wrong?"

I wanted to be careful. It was not for me to declare whether their work was flawed. Whether their readers on the porch would appreciate their story, or whether they would have been frightened by Hersh's alterations, I had no idea. I wondered whether I should simply remove Hersh's final chapter. Would it be considered a good deed or a disservice? I decided against the deletion. Hersh was entitled to his own reckoning.

"Sam wanted me to finish it for him." I hoped she'd believed me. "Hannah, would be pleased, now, I think."

Belinda rested her hand on my shoulder. "How can I help?"

I wiped my eyes with my sleeve. "Is there someone

around who could type this? And perhaps then make several copies? Of the entire stack? So they can be passed around to the others?"

"I'll type them myself, when I get home tonight," she promised. "I'm suddenly not tired." She gazed at my handwriting on the paper. "I think I can make this out. If not, I'll ask you tomorrow."

"I'll still be here," I said with a grin.

We laughed. "One more thing," I said.

"You don't have to say anything to me."

"I do. Please let me say it. I need to tell you that I'm sorry. I hope someday you can find it in your heart to forgive me. I'm a terrible man."

"Terrible men don't care for their wives and teach children for fifty years," she said. "Please don't apologize again. I won't accept it the next time." She extended her hand. "Friends?"

"Friends," I agreed, reaching for her hand.

"Can I get that plate of food for you?"

"Not food. But, do you know where Harry's computer is stored? Do you think he . . .?"

"I know exactly where it is," she said.

I arose early the following morning, neither tired from the extended evening schedule nor aching from being hunched over my table for so lengthy a period. In fact, I felt quite exuberant and contented and I happily bathed, shaved, and wheeled to the dining room for a butter-drenched breakfast.

I traveled to the porch. Just inside the doorway I stopped and examined this room where I had spent virtually the entire year. It appeared different, though I couldn't pinpoint the cause. What had enhanced my ability to see the lovely grounds or had altered my other senses and permitted a greater appreciation for the smells and the sounds that came from the window, I did not know. I was comfortable there, that much I understood. The porch with all its imperfections was a pleasant place to be, and I decided to leave it at that.

I turned to wheel to my table. There, assembled, with a full web of wires and a system of components, was Harry's computer, turned on. I looked back to the door to see whether Belinda was waiting at the desk to witness my surprise and gratitude. She wasn't there.

I pushed at my tires until I faced the screen. Belinda had left a note taped to the console:

> Abe,
>
> Instructions are in the book on the table. I don't believe it's too difficult to use. Have a wonderful time. (I'll bring you tea at 10:00. And I stayed up all night and read the book. I don't know what to say other than thank you.)
>
> See you shortly
> Your friend,
> Belinda

I began to read, touching keys as each step unfolded on the page. Belinda was right. There wasn't much more to computing than typing, at least for this function, and within minutes I was proudly pecking my way through the tutorial's practice paragraph.

After a minute, I rested. I thought of our home and the care Sarah used in decorating each room. She had preferred the Colonial style, light grays and browns for the walls. But I hadn't noticed her artfulness or at least paid much attention to her efforts. Later that afternoon I would ask Belinda for help in making my room my own.

"Ech, there it is. The son of a bitch didn't steal it," Harry grumbled.

"I should've asked first, Harry," I said. I wanted to apologize. "I should have —"

"Christ, use it. I don't want it. I just thought Hersh stole it, that's all."

"I could pay you for it."

He waved at me. "Tell me a good joke someday. We'll call it even."

The only joke I could remember popped into my head. "Two couples are sitting together at a restaurant," I began. Harry's lip curled with surprise. "The one guy, Max, says to the other, 'Mortie, if I could only remember the name of that flower out there in the foyer, I could remember this thing I wanted to tell you.' "I tried to make facial expressions suitable to the story, but my comedy was weak. "His friend Mortie says, 'Max, that's a rose.' Max slaps his forehead and turns to his wife. 'Rose, he says to her, what was it that I wanted to tell my friend Mortie?'"

Harry chuckled, and began to deal the cards. "We're even," he said. "I liked it."

Outside, the sun beamed against the trellises covering the far wall to the hospital wing. The leaves seemed to stretch toward the light.

Sarah's face appeared in my thoughts. She wore her smile, the one I remembered from the train, the one I remembered in all the years that followed.

"Good morning," I said so no one could hear. "Now let me be, for just a while."

I put my fingers on the keys. "Good morning," I repeated, though no one heard me.

I began to type.

Nearly a year had gone by, but my room at Emunah remained as bleak and barren as the day I'd arrived. I had, at one time, thought about hanging a picture of Sarah, or painting over the bleached-out square on the wall outlining where my predecessor had hung his own family portrait before he conveniently died. I never did, however. I had neither the energy nor the urgency, and since Sarah was gone, nothing seemed to matter . . .

ACKNOWLEDGMENTS

I came up with the idea for this story while visiting my great grandmother, Rose Maser, in the Jewish Home and Infirmary in Rochester, New York, when I was nine. Over the next decades I thought about it, started to write, stopped, restarted, and finally went as far as I could. I had no idea what to do next. Luckily, there were people who did.

Richard Marek edited, and showed me how to craft a story out of a tangled weave of overexuberance. Alan Eisner and his staff at Regan Communications stood by me all the way, and always made me think success was possible. David Nelson at Beaufort Books took a chance on an unknown, first-time fiction writer, and never looked back.

There were others also. Iris Tubin typed and retyped. My Dad never doubted, and though he was clearly biased, loved every version no matter how misguided. Jamie, my daughter and the smartest person I know, gently pointed out inconsistencies, and Mark, my son and biggest fan, did not share our shock when Beaufort agreed to put *Abe* into print. "I knew it all along. What's the big deal?"

Most significantly, however, while I am not religious, I do think there was something else at work here. In September of last year, my wife and best friend, and the person for whom I write, was diagnosed with a particularly virulent breast cancer. Our lives spiralled into previously unknown terrors, inconcievable treatments, and unspoken desperation. It was at our lowest ebb that we got the call that *Abe* would go to market. A moment of pure joy amid otherwise grim tidings.

Cathy has recovered, though the journey was difficult and a test of endurance. The message delivered by *Abe Gilman's Ending*, therefore, is not only "keep your dreams alive, no matter how tough the circumstances," but more importantly GET TESTED, AND GET TESTED EARLY AND OFTEN. It saved us and it can save you as well.

There are several fables in this book that I heard in Sunday School before I was Bar Mitzvahed. The story about the rabbi deceiving his captor by swallowing the paper on which "death" was written was first told to me by Mrs. Rifkin, my first Hebrew teacher. I was unable to find the source, so I apologize in advance if this tale is not properly accredited.

Also, legend has it that Emily Dickinson wrote a note to her young cousins the morning she passed away that said simply, "Called Back." Though not in her published poems, two words never better conveyed a message of hope and promise in the face of death. Here is a nod from Sarah Gilman to Ms. Dickinson.

A nod also from me to Allan Burns and Claude Klotz for the notions conveyed and the sentiments expressed on page 63 (second full paragraph).

Finally, I had this manuscript read by several Jewish scholars, a few historians, and one rabbi. Each had comments on the phonetic spellings of some of the Yiddish words. Try as I did, there were several disagreements on the formulation that were impossible to reconcile. I did my best. I hope all will forgive me.